MY FATHER'S SON

MY FATHER'S SON

BY TERRI FIELDS

Roaring Brook Press
New York

Text copyright © 2008 by Terri Fields
Published by Roaring Brook Press
Roaring Brook Press is a division of Holtzbrinck Publishing holdings
Limited Partnership
175 Fifth Avenue, New York, New York 10010
www.roaringbrookpress.com

Distributed in Canada by H. B. Fenn and Company Ltd.

Library of Congress Cataloging-in-Publication Data
Fields, Terri, 1948-
My father's son / Terri Fields. — 1st ed.
p. cm.
Summary: Kevin's life of high school classes, crushes, basketball,
and shuttling between his parents' homes falls apart when his
father is arrested as a suspected serial killer, leading Kevin to
a new understanding of his family and himself.
ISBN-13: 978-1-59643-349-6
ISBN-10: 1-59643-349-3
[1. Fathers and sons—Fiction. 2. Serial murderers—Fiction.
3. Loyalty—Fiction. 4. High schools—Fiction. 5. Schools—Fiction.
6. Family life—Arizona--Fiction. 7. Arizona—Fiction.] I. Title.
PZ7.F47918My 2008
[Fic]—dc22
2008020295

Roaring Brook Press books are available for special
promotions and premiums. For details contact:
Director of Special Marketing, Holtzbrink Publishers.

First Edition September 2008
Book design by Debora Smith
Printed in the United States of America

2 4 6 8 10 9 7 5 3 1

To Rick
To my mother who has made it so easy to be
her child, and to my children, Lori and Jeff,
who have made it so worthwhile to be a mother.

breaking news

Ten minutes. Just ten minutes, and then I'll start my pile of waiting homework. I stretch out on the sofa; Mom's not home, so feet up is okay. I press the TV remote, and ominous music with bold words, "BREAKING NEWS," fills the screen. I better pay attention. It could be good for extra credit in Government tomorrow.

I turn up the volume as a woman at a news desk announces, "This just in. In a spectacular development, the alleged DB25 Monster has been arrested. Police apprehended him trying to escape through the bathroom window of 32-year-old Joyce Garlen's apartment. Officers found Ms. Garlen bound and badly beaten, her body bearing the signature DB25 markings. As with other DB25 victims, she had allegedly been tortured and branded before being

1

left to die of her injuries. Ms. Garlen was still alive when police reached her, and she has been rushed to John C. Lincoln Hospital, where she is now in a coma. She is the eleventh known DB25 victim in the tri-state area over the past two years."

Then the camera switches from the anchor to a mug shot of the monster they caught. And it is my face—or least my face as it will look in 20 years. My same thick black hair, my same long eyelashes, my same brown eyes. A new image replaces the full-screen mug shot as I see two cops hustling a handcuffed man into the back of a police car.

chapter 1

Two weeks earlier

I AM TRYING TO PAY attention in Spanish. I swear I am. But it's almost impossible with Emily sitting only one seat ahead of me. Every day I tell myself, today's it. Today I'm going to ask her if she wants to hang out this weekend. But I don't. I guess if I don't ask, I can keep thinking she'd say yes.

Señora Noyel calls on me. I have no idea what she's asked. I'm pretty sure though that whether I answer it in Spanish or English, what I'm daydreaming about Emily is not the answer Señora wants.

"Uh . . . no comprendo," I say.

"Usted no presta la atención," says Señora Noyel.

Not true. I was paying attention . . . to Emily. Señora Noyel repeats her question and calls on someone else for an answer. I go back to my thoughts of

Emily until Señora Noyel hands out a paper and tells us to work with our partner to translate it.

The gods were smiling on me the day Señora Noyel assigned Emily as my partner for the semester, definitely the day Spanish became my favorite class. Emily moves her chair real close so we can work on the translation. Right now, it's pretty hard to concentrate because Emily smells so good, but somehow we get the paragraph finished.

Okay, now's the perfect time. I'm going to ask her out. "We're practically the first ones done," I say. "Guess we're a pretty good team." But then my mouth stops short of the date part.

"Yeah, we are a good team." Emily fixes me with her 10,000-megawatt smile and says, "Great that it's Friday, huh?"

"Sure is . . . don't know how we'd survive without weekends."

"So," she looks at me with her big blue eyes. "Are you going to hang out at Cliff's tomorrow night?"

Jason mentioned that people were going to Cliff's, but I thought it was just some guys to play a little b-ball. Suddenly, the weekend seems a whole lot more interesting. "Uh . . . you going?" I ask.

"Well . . . I thought I might if certain other people planned to go . . ." She stops speaking, but her eyes hold mine.

"Yeah, well, I might be there." I'm trying to be cool about this, but maybe that was too cool. I want to be there with her. "Yeah. Actually, I guess I'm going for sure." My voice almost squeaks. This girl turns me into pathetic.

But Emily doesn't laugh at me or roll her eyes. She just says, "Great! If you're there, it'll be lots more fun."

I grin. Life is good. After school, when Jason and I meet up, I punch his arm. "Hey," he says, "trying to disable your teammate?"

"Hey yourself," I reply. "How come you failed to mention girls going to Cliff's?"

Jason shrugs. "Guess I was waiting for you to tell me you had to stay home and study Pre-Cal, and then I was going to spring it on you to see if it changed your mind."

"Very funny." I say. "It's not like I study all the time. It's just that you never study at all."

"And I'm a better man for it," Jason proclaims.

"Yeah, but *your* dad hasn't already made plans to go to the Harvard-Yale game when he visits you at Yale."

Jason yawns. "Scottsdale Community College is fine by me. So how'd you hear about the girls?"

I shrug. I try to make it sound unimportant. "Emily mentioned it."

"Whoa!" Jason sighs. "You know, if I weren't your best friend, and you didn't have it so bad for her, I'd . . ."

I interrupt. "I don't have anything so bad for anyone."

"Great," he says. "Then you won't care if I hit on her?"

"Stay away from Emily."

Jason laughs. "Uh, huh. That's what I thought. You got it bad, my man. Well, at least you recognize a truly hot girl. Want to head over to Cliff's together?"

I shake my head. "I'm staying at my dad's this weekend. I'll probably just drive myself over."

By Saturday night, what I am driving myself is crazy. It's hard to know what girls think looks good. I stand staring at the closet. Finally, I pull on my green shirt. I go to grab the shoes I want from the closet, and I realize they're at Mom's. These loafers will have to do. Living in two places means the stuff I need is always at the other house. My clothes are minimal at Dad's since I'm only here some weekends.

I reach for my aftershave and realize that it's empty. "Great!"

Dad hears me. "Can I help with something?"

I hold up the empty bottle.

"Ahh . . . so tonight isn't about basketball with the guys, huh? You know . . . I used to use that aftershave, but I found something I think is better. Try this . . ." He brings in a dark blue bottle. "Want to tell me about her?"

I shrug. "Just a girl at school. Nothing special."

Dad grins. He knows me too well. "Yeah, well, nothing special is one lucky lady if you're interested. Have fun tonight."

I sigh. "I hope so."

Dad laughs. "I'd give you the whole every-guy-has trouble-figuring-out-girls-in high-school speech, but I think I've already done that. And as I remember, the last time I shared my great wisdom on women, you were less than impressed."

I smile. I don't remember any such conversation, but maybe I wasn't listening. I check my cell phone for the time. I don't know if it'd be better to get to Cliff's before Emily so she has to come up to me or after she's already there so it doesn't seem like I'm hanging out looking for her.

"I won't wait up for you," Dad calls as I grab my keys and head for the door. "Good luck!"

Dad's so great that way. I never have to answer a thousand questions. If this had been Mom, she'd have wanted to know if Cliff's parents would be home; she'd have asked who else was going. She'd have kept prodding me for the name of the girl I liked. Dad just keeps life simple.

Cliff lives in an old beige stucco house set back from the street. It has a huge backyard and a great blacktop area for basketball. There've been a few other times when girls have been here . . . so I don't know what the big deal is for me about tonight. Except as I think about it, the last time girls were over, I hung out playing basketball and pretty much ignored them. Of course, that was before Emily.

By the time I get to Cliff's tonight, I've got the whole sweaty palms thing. I walk into the backyard, trying to look around without being obvious. I don't see Emily, but there are a lot of people, and it's kind of dark, so it's hard not to stare and still see anything. Suddenly, I feel a sharp poke in my ribs. "Be still his beating heart, his true love isn't here."

"Knock it off, Jason!" I poke him back.

He laughs. "So . . . I guess no basketball tonight."

"Is that because you don't want to get beat?" I bluff.

"Are you kidding? Me worry about getting beat by you?"

"Not kidding, not a worry, just a fact," I say.

"Is that so?" He glances at my feet. "Nice shoes for b-ball," Jason smirks. "Looks like you got dressed for other games tonight."

I know my face is getting red, and so I shoot back, "Uh, well . . . you move so slow, I don't need basketball shoes. Truth is . . . I could be wearing flip-flops and beat you."

"Flip-flop . . . flip-flop. Is that the beating of the boy's heart when he hears about Emily?"

"Nope. Flip-flop, flip-flop; that's you on the ground after I've made a killer crossover."

I try to glance around without Jason's noticing. I don't see Emily. I could go look for her, but . . .

"I think your girlfriend may have stood you up," Jason says.

"Hey! I keep telling you, she's not my girlfriend."

"That's because she's got good taste in guys."

"Oh, like you'd know anything about that!"

Then I hear, "Want some popcorn?" I turn around to see Emily holding out a bowl to share.

"Thanks," Jason says, reaching for a handful. I'm going to kill him. Really, I am. He pays no attention to my signals and keeps talking to Emily. It takes about ten minutes before he finally gets the hint that three's a crowd and disappears. The moon is out; the night is nice, and when a slow song starts, I get up my courage and ask Emily if she wants to dance.

We join the other swaying couples up on the patio, and as I put my arms around Emily and her face leans into my shoulder, I think that life doesn't get much better. While there's part of me wishing we could be like a few of the couples really going at it on blankets over by the bushes, on the whole, it's pretty great just to talk and laugh and hold Emily's hand.

Emily seems like she's having a good time. We talk about school and TV and movies and stuff. As the party starts to break up, I blurt out, "So, I could take you home if you want. I mean . . . first we could get something to eat or something." It isn't too smooth, but at least it's out there.

Emily smiles at me. She really does have the greatest smile of any girl anywhere. "Kev . . . that sounds great, but I'm spending the night at Callie's. I've got to go home with her. I promised. It was a great idea though. I'm really sorry."

If she's sorry, I'm even sorrier. We're both sitting on this lawn chair sort of off from the crowd. I have my arm around Emily, and she's snuggled in next to me. Her cologne or something smells so good. She looks up at me, "Tonight's been nice, huh?"

I take that as my cue to lean over and kiss her. And the kiss is every bit as good as I imagined it would be.

I don't want to, but I walk Emily out to Callie's car and watch her leave. But then I start letting myself think about tonight, think about how maybe Emily might want to be more than just my Spanish partner, which me gusta muy mucho!

chapter 2

ON SUNDAY, IT'S ALMOST noon by the time I roll out of bed. I head downstairs into Dad's office looking for him. He's sitting at his computer. "Sorry," I yawn. "I didn't mean to sleep so late."

I practically trip over the mound of tossed-off shoes scattered in his office. I guess that's where I get it. Mom always gets so mad that I don't put my stuff away at her house. Dad's clothes and stuff are even messier than mine. None of the things that drive Mom crazy bother Dad. That's part of why staying at his condo is a lot more fun. I love the computer games too. Electronics geek that he is, Dad has every game a guy could want. And my room here . . . Dad doesn't care that me and my friends have graffitied one whole wall with cartoons and comments. Mom, who washes fingerprints off light covers, would freak if she ever saw my room at Dad's. But no need to worry. That will never happen.

Dad turns away from his computer, "So you ready for one of my super cheese and onion omelets for breakfast—or would that be lunch now?"

"An omelet sounds great. Extra cheese on mine." And as we start toward the kitchen, I add, "Breakfast, lunch—your omelets are the best. But aren't you the guy who said mornings should be abolished?"

Dad laughs, "True. When I retire, I'm never getting up before 10:00!"

"Yeah, sounds great to me."

"Okay, sport, but before you retire, maybe you should finish high school."

I shrug, "Yeah, too bad. I guess I better try college too."

"That'd be good," Dad says. "Then law school, then get a job, then become a partner in a big law firm, and then you're practically at retirement."

I groan. "I'll be ancient by then. "But you . . . you really could retire right now."

"Hey, I'm not that old," Dad says. "And other than sleeping late . . ."

I interrupt. "No, really, think about it. It'd be perfect. You'd never have to see your awful boss again, and if you didn't have to travel for work, I could move in. That'd make everyone happier."

Dad opens the refrigerator. "You might get real sick of pizza and omelets. Your mom feeds you better, I'm sure. As for Jared Johnston . . . I wouldn't miss working for him. But the money is good at Environ; the work's easy, and I travel enough that I don't see my boss all that much. Maybe I'll get lucky, and Johnston will retire!"

"Then you could be boss," I say.

Dad shrugs. "Don't think that'll happen in my lifetime."

"Well," I say. "It should."

Dad grins. "Maybe you'll hire me when you're in charge of that big law firm. Meanwhile, I think I better keep working at my current job. Someone has to pay for your fancy college."

"I could get a part-time job this year," I say. "I could start helping."

Dad shakes his head. "Not necessary. Believe me, you'll have plenty of time in your life to work." He pours the beaten eggs into the skillet. "Speaking of time . . . did you have a good one last night?"

"It was pretty okay," Thinking about Emily's kiss, I can't keep a stupid smile off my face.

Dad sets the omelet in front of me. "With a grin like that . . ." He laughs. "Well, that's my man."

"Yeah," I say, "I am the man! Hey, Dad, before Mom, in high school did you ever have it really bad for a girl?"

He groans. "That was such ancient history, and I'm so old, I can't even remember high school, let alone who or what I liked." I think that's not exactly true. He's talked a lot about high school sports, but maybe when it came to girls . . . he was just with Mom, and he sure doesn't like to talk about her.

Once we are finished with breakfast, Dad announces that he has the brand-new beta version of *World Revenge*, and the computer is all set up for us to play. I am super psyched. Even if his regular job as a computer expert means travel and lots of boring work, his side job as a beta tester for new computer games has been great for both of us.

It takes us about an hour to figure out how to play *World Revenge*, but then it's absolutely amazing. Dad and I are pretty evenly matched. I take over a country; then he conquers one. *World Revenge* is going to be huge, and I'm getting to play it way before most people. We play all afternoon, right through eating take-out pizza for dinner. I've just managed to get most of South America when Dad says, "It's 7:30. We've got to stop."

I hate to leave, but the custody agreement says that I have to be back at Mom's before 8:00 P.M. on

Sunday nights, and it's not worth it if I'm late. Weird thing is if it's a weekend at Mom's, I don't have to be in by 8:00, and after I get home from Dad's weekend, I can go back out, but I have to check in at Mom's by 8:00 on Dad's weekends. Makes no sense, but what kid can make any sense of their parents' divorce.

As I head for the front door, Dad calls, "Good luck with Miss Nameless!"

"That's Miss Perfect Nameless to you!" I call back.

Dad laughs. Then he comes over to me. Suddenly, he's got that serious-father look on his face. "I think it's great that you like this girl. Just remember: don't let this one or any other girl destroy your chance at Yale."

I climb into my Jeep and start home. The car is in Dad's name, but he said that was only a legal thing. From the first day he handed me the keys and let me drive it off the showroom floor, it has been my car.

I remember when we bought it. The salesman kept asking Dad questions, and he just kept saying, "Ask my son. It's his car, his decision." So I got a sound system that rocks, an eight-cylinder engine, and midnight black inside and out.

When Mom first saw the car, she said that since we live in Arizona, she wished I'd chosen white to reflect the heat. That's just the way Mom is. She can't help it, I guess. She's always worrying about something.

Man . . . if I could just live with Dad. Life would be so relaxing. Like he was okay to leave Emily as Miss Nameless. No grilling. No digging for details.

As I take my stuff in, Mom asks if I've had a good weekend. I've learned. If I say my time at Dad's was great, she gets jealous, but then she also gets pissed if she thinks Dad wasn't nice enough to me. So I always keep my answers noncommittal. "I've still got a lot of Pre-Cal," I tell her, which is true because I got none of it done at Dad's. I head into my room to get started, but my book isn't in my duffle.

Mom doesn't say anything when I tell her I have to return to Dad's. But I can see that she thinks I did it on purpose to spend more time with him.

When I get to Dad's, I pull out my key. No point in making him come to the door. He's probably still deep into *World Revenge,* and he might not even hear the bell. When Dad gets really into his computer games, I think the whole house could burn down, and he wouldn't know it.

I let myself in, head upstairs, grab the book still sitting on my unmade bed, and head back down. I'm about ready to go into Dad's office to say good-bye, but then decide I won't bother him. I'll just leave. As

I'm almost to the front door, I have a better idea. I won't disturb him, but if I sneak a peek over his shoulder, I might be able to pick up a few clues on the strategy for winning this new game before he notices I'm there. Hey, it's only fair considering all the extra practice he's getting.

I tiptoe into the office, but Dad's big computer isn't even on. Instead he's hunched over a small gray laptop I've never seen before. I creep closer. Is this a new gaming system? But when I get right behind Dad, it looks as if the screen is filled with some kind of spreadsheet. "What's that?" I ask.

Dad slams the computer shut and wheels around. "What are you doing here?"

"Uh . . . I live here sometimes?" I say.

Dad laughs. "Well, of course, you do. You just scared me."

I tell him I forgot my book and ask him about the new computer.

"Oh," he sort of keeps his hand on the closed computer. "It's nothing. Just looking it over for a friend. Now you better get going before your mom kills us both."

And he's right about Mom being mad, so I take off. I'm driving home, dreading the Pre-Cal that awaits me, but just for a minute, it kind of crosses my mind that Dad usually can't wait to show me new computer stuff. Why is he being so weird about the laptop? And then again . . . why do I care?

So my life falls into this up, down, up, down. Most of that is because of Emily. Some days, I'm sure she really likes me. Her kiss sure sent that vibe. But then on Wednesday, when I finally work up the nerve to ask her if she wants to catch a movie on Friday, she tells me she has a cousin coming in from Denver, and she's going to be busy. Couldn't she ditch the cousin for a few hours if she wanted to be with me? I think it. I don't say it. Sometimes, I'm pretty sure life was easier back in the fourth grade when I was sure all girls had cooties.

Jason says he can't see why a hot girl like Emily would ever want to be with a math geek like me when she could nestle into a cut body like his. But I assure him that cut and his body are two concepts that don't even fit in the same universe.

I'm so bogged down with Pre-Cal. I don't know why some teachers think that ten problems are better than one, and a hundred are better than ten. Good thing I've got Español. Today, in Noyel's class, I mention to Emily that maybe if she wants I could stop by her house on Saturday.

Emily smiles, "That'd be nice. Just call first to make sure I'm home."

"Yeah . . . yeah . . . I'll do that." I want to ask her what time would be best; I want to tell her I'll come over whenever she wants. But that would not be at all cool, so I don't say anything more.

Emily does that hair toss thing that girls do. "Well, then maybe I'll see you Saturday."

"Yeah, I'll give you a call." It should work perfectly! Dad's borrowed my car, but he promised he'd get it back to me by Saturday morning, which means I can still go to Emily's Saturday night. I'll have time to wash the car if I need to on Saturday afternoon, and I'll already have a full tank of gas. Dad said the gas would be my "payment" for letting him use my car for his business trip while his is in the shop. I didn't even know he'd been having problems with his Lexus.

After school Thursday, I head home promising myself at least ten minutes of tube time before hitting the homework. Lying on the sofa, I turn on the TV.

And then in one moment of breaking news, everything I thought I knew about everything falls apart.

chapter 3

I SIT IN FRONT OF the flickering television for a long time. It gets dark, but I don't turn on a light. Every 15 minutes, breaking news shows my father's face, and then another reporter refers to him as the alleged DB25 Monster. Cameras switch to the victim's apartment. Her bathroom window. Then video of two burly police officers putting Dad in a police car. He ducks his head, but there's no doubt that it's Dad. This makes no sense.

I hear the front door open. As she walks in, Mom calls, "I'm sorry I'm late. We got a last-minute batch of data to enter. Did you think to make a salad?"

I don't answer. Mom comes into the living room. "Why don't you turn on some lights? And why are you sitting here like some kind of zombie staring at the TV set?" She puts her purse down on the coffee table. "Kevin, please. I know that school is hard, and I don't mind you relaxing, but could you do a little something more around here than homework and TV watching? You know, it costs a lot to keep this household running, and I don't make the kind of money your father does."

And then, just as she mentions Dad, his face once again fills the screen. I use the remote to take it off mute, and Mom hears for herself all about the capture of the alleged DB25 Monster whose murderous reign terrorized three states. She sinks down onto the sofa next to me. "It's on all the channels every few minutes," I croak.

Mom turns from the TV and looks at me, and I can see it in her eyes—it's only for an instant, an involuntary thing—a look of absolute fear as she sees my father's son . . . the two of us as one. Then Mom covers it up and wraps her arms around me. "They're wrong, Mom," I say. "You'll see, they're wrong. We have to help Dad. I don't know why he was in that woman's apartment, but he didn't do those things. He couldn't have!"

Mom doesn't answer. We remain by the TV all night long. Food is forgotten. Who can eat? I know the awful feeling in the pit of my stomach will get better at any moment. After the next commercial . . .

after the next show . . . they're going to break in again and announce that they've made a mistake.

Instead, talking heads just keep repeating the same wrong information and congratulating themselves on a safer community. The late, late news says that they will be taking a DNA sample from Dad and checking to see if it matches scrapings from under the woman's fingernails.

Well at least they're going to do something! There won't be any match, and then this whole terrible thing will be over. I know my father. If the police found him at that woman's, it's because he was helping her, fixing her computer or something. Too bad they're wasting time with my dad when the real DB25 guy is still out there. I hope they have the DNA evidence by early tomorrow. Poor Dad. Spending a night in a jail.

"Mom, let's go to wherever they're holding Dad!"

Mom frowns. "I'm sure they wouldn't let us see him."

"Well, if we can't go to that jail, we've at least got to call the police, find out what's happening."

Mom shakes her head. "The police won't tell us anything that they haven't told everyone else. Kevin, let's just wait for one day. There's got to be some sort of logical explanation."

But I can't just wait. This is my father. I look up

the phone number for the Maricopa County Jails. An officer answers.

"I . . . uh . . . I'd like some information on the arrest of Greg Windor."

He sounds tired. "Yes, you and many, many other people, it seems. So let me repeat—all that is being released about Greg Windor will be delivered through official channels and scheduled press conferences." The line goes dead.

I slam the phone down. "Damn!"

"I tried to tell you, Kevin," Mom says. There's a deep worry crease in her forehead.

chapter 4

THE TV CONTINUES TO blare BREAKING NEWS flashes that rehash exactly the same photos and same comments for the hundredth time. Finally, Mom stands up. "I'm going to bed," she says in a flat voice. I think you should too." I can't even think about sleeping. But Mom may be right about turning off the TV. I can't see those same videos and that same mug shot of my face replayed again and again.

I trudge into my room, thinking. I don't know anything about jail. Have I ever known anyone who had a parent in prison? No. The people in our group don't do jail. My only info is from TV and movies. The real place can't be as bad, can it?

Usually, I sleep through both my morning alarms, and Mom has to wake me when she comes back from her early jogging, but not today because I actually haven't gone to sleep. I've been pacing and then lying in bed, staring at the ceiling. Finally, when after the clock has inched to 7:00 A.M., I head out to the den.

To my surprise, Mom's already there instead of out on her morning run. She's still in her bathrobe, holding the remote in one hand, staring at the TV screen and biting her lip. When she sees me, she switches the television off.

"What're you doing?" I ask.

"You don't need to see this," she says.

But I do. I wrench the remote from her hand and switch the television back on "And now an exclusive interview with Don Pelder, the Utah father of the DB25's third victim." He is a gray-haired man with gold wire-rimmed glasses. He looks as if he could be anybody's next-door neighbor.

The interviewer says, "I know you've been waiting for this day for a long time."

The man nods vigorously. "You can't know how much. Every man on the street, I scrutinize and wonder if *he's* the one. My daughter's never been the same since that beast tried to end her life. And our Kimmie, what did she ever do to deserve the things he did to her?"

The man's voice breaks, and the screen is filled

with the photo of a pretty college girl with dark hair and smiling eyes, dressed in a track uniform and holding a trophy. The father's voice continues over the photo, "He left my daughter not only physically brutalized, but terrified every minute of every day."

The interviewer says something about how sorry she is. The man nods. He stares straight into the camera. "If I could, I'd like to be the one to kill that monster. I'd make it happen real, real slow and real, real painful."

The screen switches back to the announcer with another mug shot of Dad. And in a solemn voice, she announces that the most recent victim is still in a coma in critical condition. Then she says they'll be right back with another exclusive interview from another victim's family member. I think I'm going to throw up.

Mom leaves the remote in my hand, but she gets up and unplugs the set. "Kevin, listen to me. These people . . . they're in pain, and they're speaking from their pain. They're talking about the man who did these things to their families. But they don't know that that man is your father. He hasn't been convicted of any crime yet. Things will calm down. They will." I don't know if she's telling herself or me.

"Mom, we've got to go to that jail and figure out how we can help him get out of this nightmare."

"No, Kevin," she says, "I've been thinking all night. I know it's hard, but going to that jail is about the last thing we should do. Your dad can and probably already has hired a good lawyer. If he wants you or even me, the lawyer will let us know. Your father is very smart. You know that. He'd get us there if he needed us. If he doesn't, our going could only give him more problems. He has enough to deal with."

I storm out of the den. Mom is always too scared to do anything. So I don't care what she says. I won't just sit here and let the world trash my father.

Mom follows me upstairs to my room. "Kevin, please. There's nothing we can say or do to make them release your father."

"I can tell them he's the best dad ever." My voice is ragged.

Mom has tears running down her cheeks. "I'm sure he is a great dad. But, sweetheart, I don't think that will free him."

"Yeah? Then what will?" I'm trying not to cry myself.

Mom bites her lip. "Well . . . they say DNA can prove things, and the reports state that they have your Dad's DNA. The police will process it. We just have to try to be patient." Mom reaches out to me, but I pull away.

I don't go down to the jail. I tell myself it's because I believe my mother. Yet part of me wonders if it's because I'm just too chicken, or if the real reason I don't go to see Dad in jail is because I'd have to admit that this nightmare is real.

I start getting ready for school, pretending that it's a normal day and the whole thing with Dad was only a bad nightmare. Then Mom knocks on my door, and I open it. She tries to smile, but I see she's twisting her hands together. "How about playing hooky from school today?"

"Are you kidding?" I ask. "Why? What just happened now?"

Mom shakes her head. "Nothing. I just think it would be a good idea if you'd stay home."

"Really, nothing else happened?" I have an urge to run down and turn on the TV.

Mom shakes her head. "Not that I know of."

"And you?" I say. "Are you staying home too?"

Mom shakes her head no.

I start yelling, "Then why should I stay home and hide?" I don't even know if I want to go to school. I just want to scream at someone. "You never make any sense."

Mom doesn't scream back. "It's different," she says. "I use my maiden name. At work, they don't know I was married to your dad." She puts her hand on my shoulder. "I remember high school, Kevin. They'll know you're his son, and kids can be so cruel. Let things settle down a bit." Mom bites her lip. "I'm worried about you."

"I'm fine!" I say, even though I'm not. "It's Dad we should be worried about."

Mom tries another tack. "Tell you what. I'll take the day off too. We'll stay home and watch daytime TV together. When's the last time we ever did that?"

I think *never*. She must really be desperate for me to stay home. Mom is always short on money, and after the bad flu she had, she doesn't have any paid sick days left. I calm down enough to feel bad for her, and maybe I even worry a little that she's right in saying I should stay away. "Okay, I'll stick around today. But you go to work; I'll be all right."

Mom seems so relieved. "Thanks."

I shrug, "Hey, it means no Pre-Cal. How can that be bad?"

There's a catch in Mom's voice as she tells me, "You're . . . you're the best son. You remember that." She reaches up, kisses me on the cheek, and then she is gone.

Now, I have a day off to do nothing; I have no one

to nag me about chores; I can watch stupid daytime TV; I don't even have any unfinished homework looming. And yet, I'd rather be taking the worst of Mrs. M.'s Pre-Cal tests or slaving over a hundred of her impossible problems than spending one more hour alone here.

When Mom gets home that evening, she's not much company. There's nothing new about Dad. All weekend, our drapes stay shut. We don't leave the house. We don't talk about Dad, and we can't talk about anything else. Neither of us wants to watch anymore terrible TV, and yet we leave it on.

Saturday morning—we hold our breath as a reporter announces a special report. "Next! Startling new information about the DB25 Monster in our interview with Greg Windor! He's here, live in our studio, right after this commercial break. Stay tuned."

My dad. My dad is going on television. My dad is going to explain this whole thing to the world and to me. The police must have released him.

I cannot take a deep breath. Will these stupid ads ever end. "Come on!" I croak at screens of breath mints, cars, and dancing vegetables. Finally, bold black letters on the screen as a voice-over states, "We bring you this special report, live and exclusive, only on Fox 10.

Then there's a guy in the studio with the reporter. Under the guy's name, it says Greg Windor. But he's tall, and he has blond hair. He doesn't look anything like my dad. The guy starts talking. He says he's gotten a hundred calls—had to take his phone off the hook. He wants everyone to know that he isn't *that* Greg Windor. Says he hopes they fry that fiend, but to leave him alone.

Breaking news bulletins keep interrupting programs screaming, "The climate of fear and terror ends as the DB25 Monster is caught."

The only voices in our house all weekend come from the TV. Our phone is strangely silent. None of the ordinary insulting calls from Jason. No one nagging me to come play b-ball. No calls for Mom either. It's like some sci-fi thing, where maybe the world stopped, and we're the only ones alive.

I check my cell for messages a bunch of times. Once I even start to text Jason. But he hasn't called me all weekend. So either he's real busy or he's staying away. I hang up. I think I'll call Emily instead. We don't have to talk about Dad. She probably doesn't even know. I bet she's ticked that I didn't call or come over on Saturday night. I could just say it was because I had the flu. That's why I was absent on Friday too. Nah. I can barely talk to Emily even when everything is perfect. How can I do it now?

Finally, I decide to call a police station again. I need some answers. I try a different one than before. A woman answers. I ask for details about when Greg Windor might be released. She tells me the arrest didn't come out of her precinct. I start to dial another precinct and then I think, *What if the police ask who I am, and they start asking me questions about Dad? What if I say the wrong thing and make things worse for him?* I put the phone down. Maybe Mom's right. Dad will find a way to get hold of me when he wants me to say something.

The Sunday paper plops in front of our door. I bring it in. A huge black headline reads: THE MONSTER AMONG US. There is a big picture of Dad. There are more articles, besides the one on the front page. Inside there are also more photos of Dad, including the one from his high school yearbook that could be my twin. The articles are careful to keep referring to Dad as *alleged*, but all the people interviewed make it sound like they've got their guy. On the front page is a big color picture of Dad in handcuffs. He looks confused. On the inside is another picture of Dad in a black suit and the paisley tie I gave him for his birthday. He is sitting at his desk at Environ Computers. He looks perfectly normal. But you don't notice that. All you see is the big bold quote in the middle of the story. It almost forces your eyes to go right to it. "I'm in shock realizing that I sat next to this depraved monster at work and never knew it." Coworker Alexandra Lenar.

I make myself read the whole story. It's awful. The article says, "Jared Johnston, senior supervisor at Environ Computers, indicated that the company would be cooperating fully with police and extended its sympathy to all the DB25 victims. Johnston said that while the company had absolutely no idea of Greg Windor's alleged activities, personally, he had always found Mr. Windor to be aloof and a bit strange."

"Aloof? Strange!" I'm furious. How about brilliant and hardworking? Where are those words in the article? And, of course, Johnston didn't mention the credit he took for Dad's work, like the time Dad found a code error in the AlphaOmega program. He reported it to Johnston, who turned it in as his own discovery. Dad was plenty ticked, especially after there was a write-up in *Computer* magazine about Johnston's great detective work. Stupid old Johnston—who's going to do his work *now*?

And Alexandra Lenar, if she's really my dad's coworker, she must know him, and she's got to realize this can't be true.

The article says that the authorities will wait to convene a grand jury until the DNA has been processed. What takes so long for DNA test results? Don't people work on weekends?

I tear the page from the newspaper and shred it into little pieces.

chapter 5

MONDAY. I'M STILL HIDING out at home. I
haven't slept, and I'm so tired. I wonder if I
could just pull the covers over my head and never
get out of bed again. Mom doesn't have to beg me to
stay home; I seem to have lost the ability to move.

By noon, the silence is deafening. My unwilling
feet find their way to the den, and my hand flicks
the remote to hear a news conference. The FBI guy
and the police officer who arrested Dad come out
on a stage. There are so many news people there. I
don't think that many show up for the president.
They are shouting questions and pointing cameras.
One reporter screams, "Does this mean that people
can leave their windows open and sleep safely at
night now?"

And more reporters chime in, "Why did he choose

these communities?" "How did he target his victims?"

The men on the stage wait for silence. The FBI guy goes first, saying that he'll begin by summarizing what they know about the DB25 Monster. The agent talks of the 11 known victims in 3 states, but given the signature, it's possible that there are more. "We are unclear at this time as to what the *DB* stands for. However, we will continue to investigate this. It is possible that the *25* relates to the number of victims, but this, too, is still under investigation."

A local police lieutenant takes over, explaining again how the officers broke into Joyce Garlen's apartment, finding her unconscious in the living room, bound, beaten, and branded with DB25 markings. Hearing noises, officers ran to the bathroom, where they saw my dad climbing out of the window. "Initially, Mr. Windor has been charged with trespassing. We expect further charges to be filed shortly."

The reporters shout question after question.

"Has Windor talked? What's he saying?"

"Did he have the mask on him that the victims tell us DB25 uses?"

"Do the doctors think this latest victim will live? Do they think she'll come out of her coma? Is there brain damage?"

"Have the DNA results come back yet?"

The police don't answer any of these questions. In fact, they only announce that the victim is still in ICU, where she remains alive but unconscious with grave injuries. They promise another news conference as soon as there is any further information to report.

By Monday night, I don't know what I should be doing, but I do know I can't sit around waiting anymore. When Mom gets home, I tell her to sit down. "Mom, I've made up my mind. I've got to go to wherever they're keeping Dad."

Mom starts twisting her hands. "Kevin, please. We've already agreed that this wouldn't be a good idea. Please think it through."

"*We* didn't decide anything. You did. And now, I'm deciding, and I'm going."

Mom says, "Wait. You can see how the reporters pounce on any scraps to create more breaking news. Look at what a big thing they made of that interview with the other Greg Windor." She takes a deep breath. "Kevin, do *not* go down to that jail—at least not yet."

I pace back and forth. "You don't care about Dad or me," I shout. "I . . . I know why you don't want me there. You just don't want anyone to connect

Dad to me because I live with you, and if I start being part of the story . . . so will you! You only care about yourself."

Mom recoils as if I'd hit her. She wipes away tears. "Kevin, I can't physically stop you from going. I can't even stop you from camping out in front of that jail. But you're wrong—so wrong when you say I don't care about you. You are the center of my life."

I don't tell anyone this . . . not even Mom, but I can't stop thinking about the way Dad said he needed to borrow my car because he had to go out of town on business. So if he was supposed to be in some other city, then why was he found in that woman's apartment only a few miles from his own condo?

Dad and me . . . we don't keep secrets from each other. We never have, so why not tell me the truth about the car? So maybe . . . maybe I shouldn't go rushing off to see Dad yet. Maybe I don't understand about everything, but whatever this is about, he could have trusted me. I still trust him.

So if it's really true that I trust him, and I believe this will end, I should go back to school. When Dad gets out of jail, he shouldn't have to be disappointed in me because I let my grades fall while I was sitting at home not believing that he'd be freed.

It's sure quiet here. I haven't heard from Jason at all—not even one text message or IM. So even though I'm without wheels for tomorrow, I'm not calling him for a ride. As for my car—it might still be in Dad's garage, or maybe the police took it. Well, I'll see how it is with Jason at school. If it's okay, maybe I'll ask him to drive me over to Dad's place to see if my car's there.

School's not that far. So the next morning I tell myself it's good exercise to jog there. As I run, I think kids at Chapparal High know me; they're not like those scum reporters looking for any kind of scandalous story. Besides, unless it's assigned, who really pays any attention to the news?

But as the school comes into view, my heart is practically pounding out of my chest. I pass some kid I don't know on the sidewalk. Is he staring at me? "Hey," he says and moves on.

I realize he probably doesn't even know me. He was just being friendly as he passed by. I've got to stop fixating. Just because my world has fallen apart doesn't mean anyone else even knows or cares.

It feels weird not to enter from the parking lot, but actually, I'm earlier than when I drive. I open the big brown entrance doors and walk into school. There's a lot of whispering. I can feel my face getting red.

I force my feet to keep moving. I tell myself just get to Junior Hall, where the people know me; then it will be different. They'll treat me just the way they always have. With relief, I turn the corner to *our* section of the school. But the noisy hallway becomes silent. Kids I've known since kindergarten pretend not to stare. I feel like a freak in a sideshow. *Get your popcorn, get your soda, see the son of a monster.*

Only the teachers seem unaware. Inside the classroom, Mr. McBee still drones on about unknowns in Chemistry. Mr. Leonard reminds us to keep writing in our journals. In Spanish, Señora Noyel tells us to turn to our partner and practice our dialogues. I move my desk closer to Emily. "Hola, let's get this thing done muy fasto," I say, trying to keep everything normal.

Emily sort of looks away from me and says that Beth and she are partners now. "But you can't stand Beth," I say. Emily won't even look at me.

I glance around the room for a partner. Señora Noyel hurries up to me. "You're going to be Billy Rathman's partner now, but he's absent today, so you can work with me."

chapter 6

S **TILL NO WORD ON** the DNA. How long can it
take to test it? On TV, it all happens in an hour.
In real life, it seems to be taking forever. Joyce
Garlen is still in a coma, so she can't explain that my
dad wasn't her attacker. And the media is still cover-
ing this like there is no other story in the world. So
far, all the talk is about supposed motives of "this
monster." Nothing about the monster's family . . .
but Mom's worried that the press will come.

In Spanish, Emily continues ignoring me. How
can she pretend that night at Cliff's never happened?
I'm sure some idiot has just scared her to death. I
might be scared myself if I believed all the crap on
TV about my dad. I really need to be able to talk to
her. Unfortunately, Emily has a group around her all
the time, and I don't want to have a conversation in

front of her friends. Then I hear Señora Noyel tell Emily that she can make up a missed quiz after school. I remember that quiz on the conjugation of *hacer*. It won't take long, and it could be my chance to talk to Emily without her crowd around.

After school, I duck into the alcove by Señora Noyel's room and wait. "Emily," I say when she comes out of Spanish, "We need to talk."

She won't even look at me. "I can't," she says. "I promised my parents. Please, Kevin . . ." Just like that she starts to walk away.

"Wait," I put my hand on her wrist to stop her. I want to explain how ridiculous this all is. Suddenly, I feel my arm being grabbed so hard it practically cuts off my circulation. This guy I've only seen a few times, I don't even know his name, gets in my face.

He says, "Hey, Junior, stay away from the girls at this school. Police got your daddy. Now, we'll take care of you. Everybody's on to your little family of weirdos . . ." The pressure on my arm gets even harder. It feels like it's going to snap. I am not a person who fights. It doesn't accomplish anything, and it looks like it could really hurt. But then I feel a punch land on my shoulder and another hit my stomach, and I decide to throw myself at this guy. He's bigger, but the fact that my whole life has just completely fallen apart, that no one wants to believe that my dad is innocent, that Emily won't even think about the kind of person I am, makes me pound and kick at this guy like some kind of maniac. I think he's hitting me back, but I don't feel anything at all. I'm so mad, I just want to keep beating on something until some of the pain goes away.

At first, I didn't even feel all the hands pulling me and that guy apart. I could hear people shouting, but the pounding in my own ears kept their words from making sense. Then my face was smashed into the floor in some kind of wrestling hold, and then I was sitting on the floor, and then I was walking to the dean's office with two coaches on either side of me. Someone handed me a towel, and I put it up to my face. When I took the towel away, it was bloody.

They took me into the nurse's office. She sighed, "Ah guys, it's too late in the day for a fight!"

She sat me down on a cot, put on some latex gloves, and talked as if I wasn't even there. "I don't think he'll need stitches, but his mother may want to have this cut above the eye checked. He's definitely going to have two black eyes and his nose may be broken, but I can't be sure." I guess she cleaned me up some and took me to a bench right outside the dean's office. I was sort of out of it. I had no idea what had happened to the other guy or what was going to happen to me. I only knew that places I didn't realize I had on my body were beginning to hurt. They handed me a notebook and a pen and told me to write down my side of what had happened. But the knuckles on my right hand were swelling up, and my eyes were too blurry to see very well. I just put the paper down and leaned my head against the bench.

The door to the dean's office was open, and the guy I'd fought with was inside. I could hear him loud and clear. He was shouting, "If the damn school is going to let a pervert like that roam around, I should get a medal not a suspension for taking him out."

Scraps of Dean Kenter's comments about the kid's inappropriate language, my clean record, the number of fights he'd been in. I only caught pieces of what she was saying. She wasn't nearly as loud as the kid.

His voice boomed. "Oh, yeah. You're handling it. Then how come he was trying to pull that girl down an empty hallway into where no one could see her? How are you handling that? Wait'll I tell people that you're helping Monster Junior stay at our school."

I didn't hear what Dean Kenter said to that. But as the guy walked out of her office, I could tell, even through my really battered eyes, that he looked terrible. He was twice my size and I had still done some damage. It made my own pain seem worth it. "Five days," the dean said following him. "I don't want to see you back on campus until then, and, George, I don't care what your reasons are. This is your fourth fight this year . . . one more, and you're looking at expulsion."

"Yeah, sure," George said. "Why don't you ask the girl if she's glad I fought him. Ask her if it would have been better for me to let him finish marking her up with DB25 after he . . ."

"George," the dean interrupted. "That's enough. Out!"

I got called in next. The questions started. "Exactly why were you stalking Emily?"

Stalking . . . me? The room started to blur. I leaned back in the chair and let my swollen eyes close.

I'm not sure when my mom got there. I heard her pleading with Dean Kenter that I was a really good kid. I'd never been in any kind of fight. Emily and I had been friends. My record was good—I was even in the National Honor Society.

I faded in and out. Somehow, Mom got me into the car. I don't remember too much else about Friday night.

Saturday came and went, and I was pretty out of it. Mom came in, gave me pain stuff she'd gotten from the doctor, and I slept. I didn't think about Dad all day. I couldn't think about anything. It felt good.

Sunday afternoon, I tried getting up out of bed and walking around. It was like someone was driving spikes into me every time I moved. But my vision had cleared enough to see that Mom had huge black circles under her eyes. She looked awful. "Kevin," she said warily, "I know you're upset. But tomorrow, you can't go to your school. Not for any reason. Promise me."

I looked at her questioningly, and she said, "You signed a paper saying you could be expelled if you were on school premises at all during your five-day suspension, remember?"

Actually, I didn't really remember signing a paper. I didn't remember too much from the dean's office. I was trying to think, but Mom misinterpreted my silence. "Please! Dean Kenter has tried to be nice. She could have expelled you for stalking, but she didn't. She said you had always been an excellent student before all this with your dad, and it had to be hard for you now."

"What . . . having my father accused of being a sadistic murderer and me the same monster? How could she think that might be upsetting?"

Mom bit her lip, and her eyes filled with tears.

"Okay, Mom, I won't go to school. Don't worry. It'll be okay, " I said, though I didn't believe it for even a minute.

Everyone else goes to school on Monday, and I begin my suspension. I stay home and watch daytime TV. *The Jerry Springer Show* is ridiculous. It's got to be actors playing people. And the TV soaps—I'd say they're too stupid . . . well, except I guess I'm in the middle of a real-life one.

I try not to stare in a mirror at the mess that is my face, and hope each new newscast will bring word of my dad's innocence.

Jason has finally text messaged a few times. "U ok?" "U up for b-ball?" "Want me to stop by?"

I've texted back, "Yes, no, no." I'm not exactly in the mood for company.

The homework Mom requested from school sits untouched. It feels as if it belongs to some other kid in some other world. I talk to the TV, pretending I care about the contestants on the *The Price Is Right*. It beats thinking about the real people in my own life.

"Hey, buddy, you're spinning too hard. You'll never make it into the showcase showdown." The contestant doesn't listen to me. Now, he's out of the prize money. I've only been watching this game show a few days, but if I can figure how hard they should spin, why can't the people on the show? Maybe their adrenaline gets going when they see the camera.

Speaking of adrenaline, I found that George guy's picture in last year's yearbook. The guy is huge. I can't believe I actually held my own.

For the first time since the fight, I can feel my nose run. The doctor said that my nose wasn't broken, but today's the first day I think I actually believe him. I don't believe much of what anyone says anymore. Like if my dad really does have a lawyer, why haven't I heard from him? I'm done just waiting. I go to the computer and Google my dad's name with the word *lawyer*. I click on the first Web site that shows up. Apparently, Dad does have a lawyer—Rodney L. Baron. I plug Baron's name into Google. He went to Stanford Law School, has been in practice for 12 years, specializes in criminal law. Stanford . . . well . . . that's good, right? Then why hasn't the guy called me to talk to me, to help my dad?

I remember we had a debate in Government one time about whether lawyers should be allowed to write books about their own cases. A guy in my class said it was all about freedom of speech, but this girl argued that lawyers shouldn't be allowed to profit that way. It might change their whole strategy about the case. She talked about O.J. Simpson and how because his case became so well known, his lawyers became famous and made millions writing books. Maybe this guy thinks my dad's going to turn him into a superstar.

I search for Baron's name on Yahoo, and a few seconds later, I'm looking at a phone number. My mouth feels so dry. What do I say to the guy? I force my fingers to dial. A woman answers the phone with a law firm of twenty names long ended by a "How may I help you?" I chicken out and hang up.

I slam my hand against the wall. It hurts big time. I guess my fingers haven't healed. I pick up the phone again. Someone has to hurry this DNA thing along. Even if he isn't busy making movie deals for himself, this Rodney L. Baron hasn't gotten my dad freed and home. That's for sure. I dial again, wait for the laundry list of names, and ask for Mr. Baron.

But the receptionist wants to know, "Whom shall I say is calling?" I don't want to tell her. I just want to talk to Mr. Baron, and that's what I say.

She gets real frosty. "I'm sorry, but Mr. Baron is quite busy. If you care to leave your name and the nature of your business . . ." She lets her voice trail off.

I tell her that I'll just call back later. When would be a good time?

She won't tell me. No wonder my dad isn't getting out of jail. He's dealing with idiots. I slam down the phone.

That'll show her! It feels good until I stop and think about how my great performance accomplished absolutely nothing. I hit the redial on the phone. The same receptionist . . . the same laundry list of names. This time after the how can she help, I say, "It's me again. I need to speak to Mr. Baron about. . ." I take a deep breath, "Greg Windor."

"I'm sorry, Mr. Baron has no comment to make on that subject." She recites it as if she's said it a million times.

So I call back a third time. I'm sure that when I finally let loose with the truth that I am my father's son, Mr. Baron will hurry to the phone right away. I am wrong. Ms. Dragon-Lady Receptionist informs me that Mr. Baron is with clients. She adds, "Information will be released to the press as it becomes available."

"But I'm not the press. Are you deaf? I just told you I am Greg Windor's son. Do you get that?"

She says, "I understand perfectly. So far, we've

had seven of Mr. Windor's mothers, four or five wives, and more than a dozen of his brothers and sisters contact us. Oh, yes, and a daughter and two grandsons. So, sir, if you're trying to get unauthorized information, it won't work, and your ruse isn't even original. Please save yourself and this firm some time."

chapter 7

THERE'S ONLY ONE SURE way to prove I'm not
some nosy newsman looking for a scoop. And
that is why after my mother leaves for work, I find
myself waiting for the route 72 line that will take me
downtown.

The bus is mostly empty. A man a few seats ahead
of me is singing to himself, and an old woman is sitting across from me with a pink hat and little white
gloves. She looks like one of the characters from the
sitcoms on Nick at Nite. There are three guys a few
seats ahead of me who don't look much older than
me, and they're all talking to each other in Spanish.
That's it. We're the only riders. Usually, I'm driving
and trying to not be in the lane behind the bus when
it stops to let passengers on or off.

I remember once passing a big city bus in our

car, and my dad mentioned something about how strange the world was that most kids today had been on an airplane but never a city bus. Wonder if he could ever have predicted what has prompted my first bus ride.

By the time we reach downtown, only the pink-hatted lady and I are left. I signal for my stop, and the bus pulls over to let me off near a tall building of glass that reaches up into the sky. 414 . . . it's the right address.

I take a deep breath and open the glass doors. There's a tall courtyard with a skylight at the top and a shining marble floor that someone must have to polish all the time. It must cost a lot to have an office in this building. I press the gleaming brass button by the elevator door. It leaves a smudge.

I step into a plush green carpeted elevator that zips to the fourteenth floor so fast that I'm a little dizzy. The elevator opens, and I'm in the law office. There's no door to open or anything. How did my dad even know about this place?

The same snotty receptionist is on the phone at the front. I recognize her voice. I walk up to her and ask to see Mr. Baron.

She starts to ask me if I have an appointment. Then she stares at me and takes a deep breath. I stare right back even though my heart is pounding.

I hope my voice won't crack as I say, "I tried to tell you yesterday that I am Greg Windor's son." I take out my school ID. Her eyes never leave my face. "Now, can I see Mr. Baron?"

When she answers me, she doesn't sound so sure of herself anymore. She asks me to wait right here . . . not to go anywhere . . . just to wait. "My God, you look just like . . ." She stops herself. "How old are you?"

I don't answer. I sit down on the brown leather sofa. For 30 minutes I stare at the covers of some glossy magazines, but I have no idea what they say. I am getting more nervous the whole time, but finally the receptionist motions me toward an office door. "Right in there," she says. "I . . . I'm sorry I didn't believe you before."

I've been trying to think what the man who will free my dad would look like, but he's nothing like what I'd expected. He's short with graying hair and a trimmed mustache, and he's wearing a crisp white shirt and a perfectly knotted black tie. He ushers me into his office without saying a word, motioning me to a blue leather chair on the other side of his big oak desk. I have to step around stacks of papers to get to the chair. If my dad's DNA results are buried in those piles, his lawyer might never find them. Mr. Baron sits down at his desk, and his chair squeaks a little. We stare at each other for a minute. I keep waiting for him to say something. Maybe it's some sort of lawyer trick, but he just keeps silently looking at me.

I take a deep breath. "I don't think you're doing enough to get my dad out of jail. Why is it taking so long?" I've promised myself I'm not going to let him dismiss me like I'm just a kid, so I add, "My dad sent me to find out."

Mr. Baron has steel-blue eyes that just kind of cut through a person. "Your dad sent you, huh?"

"That's right, he's mad because the DNA thing is taking so long. They said on the news there were scrapings under the woman's nails, and they could get DNA from that."

Mr. Baron just keeps staring at me. It feels awful. "Well . . . when are you getting the results?" I try sitting up a little straighter in my chair so I'll look bigger.

"Your dad didn't send you to see me," Mr. Baron says.

"Yes, he did!" I lie.

Mr. Baron says, "Even if you are his son and not just a paparazzi look-alike, I can't discuss his case with you. So I'll tell you what, I'll let your dad know that you came by. If you are his son, and if he wants to get in touch with you, we'll make it happen. Meanwhile, you can rest assured that I'm doing all that I can for him."

I want to say so much more, but somehow, I let Mr. Baron shake my hand and usher me out of his office. I stand at the bus stop to go home, angry with myself for letting him get rid of me so easily. The guy had to be lying. No way my dad wouldn't have told his lawyer all about me.

There hasn't been anything in the news about my dad for two days. No call back from the lawyer either, but I'll bet Mr. Baron doesn't even work on weekends. Poor dad, sitting in some jail cell.

If I don't hear from Mr. Baron on Monday, I'll . . . I'll call him again. I won't let him bully me. I'm sure my dad told him all about me because he talks about me to everyone; sometimes, it's almost embarrassing he's so proud of me. I lie on my bed tossing and catching a baseball as I think. Why is this lawyer lying to me? What's he got to gain? But what if the lawyer isn't lying and my dad really didn't tell him about me?

If only I could talk to Dad. He's the one who always helps me make sense of stuff. I decide to talk to him now even though I know it's stupid, and he can't possibly answer. "Dad," I say. "I know you aren't a killer. Remember when we went fishing, and I caught my first trout? You took it off the hook and released it. You couldn't even kill a stupid fish."

I wipe my eyes. I'm in such a bad way that I actually decide maybe I'll voluntarily clean up my room. Usually, when my mom complains about the mess, I just sweep everything under the bed. That's where all my notebooks from last year live. I pull out the stuff to throw away. I should just toss it all, but I find the essay I did on O. Henry's use of the surprise ending, and the lab report on copper and nitric acid, and the World History paper on Dreyfus. I got an A+ on that. I slaved over it, but I barely remember it. I start rereading parts, and then I toss it down. "That's it!"

I rush to find Mom. She's in the kitchen peeling carrots. "Mom!" I say. "Sometimes, when something can't be true, it just isn't."

Mom stops peeling. "Slow down. What are you talking about?"

"Alfred Dreyfus!" I say.

She looks at me blankly. "Okay. Is he a friend of yours?"

"No, you know. The Dreyfus Affair! Dad's just like that."

Mom looks shocked. "Your father is like someone who had an affair?"

"No. Not that. Alfred Dreyfus. He was in the army in France in the 1800s."

Mom still looks confused. "And that makes him like your dad?"

"They convicted him of treason; they sentenced him to life in prison, but here's the scary part. Even when they found out the evidence against him was false, the government tried to cover it up. See what I mean?"

Mom has put the carrot peeler down. She is staring at me. "Your father isn't being accused of treason."

I can't wait for her to figure it all out. I plunge forward. "Just listen. What if Dad was only visiting Joyce Garlen when the real DB25 Monster broke in? He only kills women, but suddenly, he sees Dad there. So the DB25 drugs Dad and locks him in the bathroom. Then the DB25 Monster attacks poor Ms. Garlen and takes off. The police come, and there's Dad."

"But, Kevin, couldn't your dad explain that to the police?"

"No!" I say forcefully. "He couldn't."

"Why not?" she asks.

"Because," I answer.

Mom looks at me. She shrugs helplessly. "I don't know. I don't really see how you got all that from Dreyfus."

Dad would understand if he were here. Mom just doesn't get logical comparisons. "They're the same because police can arrest the wrong man. They can try the wrong man. They can convict the wrong man. Everyone wants the DB25 killer caught. Everyone is scared to go out because of him. And suddenly, there's Dad. The police can arrest him and say the crime is solved. So even if they discover it's a mistake, just like with Dreyfus, they're not going to tell."

Mom takes a deep breath and scratches her head. "Kevin, I don't know what to say to you. I don't think your dad did those awful things, but I don't know about this theory you have. I'm not sure what your father was doing trying to climb out of that bathroom window."

"Mom, weren't you listening? I just explained why." I'm practically shouting. "He's not guilty! He's got to be so scared. Maybe those DB25 drugs never wore off, and Dad doesn't even know who he is or that he didn't do those horrible things. But I know."

Mom reaches over to hug me and sighs, "Kevin, life is not so simple."

Why I even try to talk to my mom is beyond me. I head back into my room. I've got to get in to see my father. Either his lawyer is part of this whole conspiracy against Dad, or the drugs the DB25 gave him caused a permanent amnesia. Either way, I can't help Dad unless I see him face-to-face. So Monday, I'm going back to that lawyer, and this time, I'm not leaving until he takes me to the jail and gets me in to see my father.

Suspension over. I'm supposed to go back to school today. Mom knocks on the door to my room before I'm even out of bed. "On the counter I left you some lunch money for the week." She doesn't mention that since seventh grade, it's been my dad who's always given me my spending money.

"I'm okay," I say, even though my finances are not in good shape. It's probably wrong, but I usually spend all my money and am down to nothing by the end of the month, so Dad always makes sure my allowance is "refreshed" by day one of the following month. Only we've started a new month, and Dad's not exactly in a position to be handing out allowances. I'm not sure what we're going to do about money. Mom's worried about it, so it's another topic we don't really discuss. Seems we avoid more than we say.

My mom's signed up for every overtime hour available. She says there are some rumors starting about who she really is, and it spooks people. It's crazy. Mom's been the employee of the month twice. Why would they fire her for being married a long time ago to Dad? But who knows? Look what happened with me and Emily. So maybe Mom's work really would fire her.

"Kev . . ." Mom opens the door to my room. "I hope today's not too tough, but hang in there. I know you can. Just don't react to anything anyone says. You can't get suspended again. Dean Kenter said that the social worker would be glad to meet with you and help you. Maybe you should talk to her."

"I don't need a social worker!"

"Don't get angry. I just want you to know that she's there if you do."

"Okay, but I don't need any social worker. I just need for Dad to be freed."

Mom lingers in the doorway, " Kevin, you can't fight your dad's battles. Please try to focus on taking care of yourself."

I tell Mom okay, but she is wrong. I can and I will fight my father's battles. He would do it for me in a heartbeat. If I were the one in jail, he'd get me out, and somehow, I'll do the same for him.

There's no point in upsetting Mom any more. The hate callers who've found our phone number have already done a nice job of that. So I'll do what I need to, but Mom doesn't have to know about it right now.

It's not much of disguise, but I put on a baseball cap and pull the brim down before I head for the bus stop and take the now familiar route back to the lawyer's office. The bus is more crowded today. I guess that Mondays are busier. There's a guy in the seat in front of me reading the newspaper. I'm already over the novelty of riding the bus, and it's a long ride. I try to read over his shoulder. I lean in a little, hoping he'll turn to the sports section. Instead I see a full page article about my dad, with a picture of him from work. It's like my own face is staring back at me. I bend my head, pull my baseball cap down a little more, and look out the window. I can feel my stomach flip-flopping. But I guess no one really looks at you on the bus because I make it to the stop without any comment.

Back in the lawyer's building, I clomp across the marble floor, smear the shiny brass elevator button, and punch 14. The door opens, and the receptionist looks up. I walk right past her. "Say, wait," she calls after me. "You can't just go beyond the reception area without . . ." I don't hear the rest. I jog down the hall, not wanting anyone to stop me, and push open the door to the lawyer's office. What if he's not even there? I guess I haven't exactly thought this through, but he looks up from behind his desk really startled. "Why don't you just tell me the truth!" I demand.

He looks a little scared, like maybe he thinks I'm

the son of a mass murderer or something. I see his Adam's apple bob, but his voice comes out clear and strong. "I have told you the truth."

"Right," I say. "Okay . . . suppose you have. But not all of it. Does my father have amnesia?"

"What?" Mr. Baron either doesn't know or he's a great faker.

"Amnesia from the drugs," I repeat.

Mr. Baron shakes his head, "I don't think we need to worry about any drugs or amnesia." He makes it sound as if he's talking to a ten-year-old.

I point my finger at him. "Don't think you can just dismiss me today like I'm just some dumb kid. I am going to help my father; I'm not giving up and letting you send me away again."

The lawyer shakes his head ever so slightly. "Look, Kevin is it? I was going to have my secretary call you later and ask you to come back and see me. We can set up an appointment, but right now, I've got an important meeting that I'm already late for."

"A meeting?" I can hear my voice rising. "Are you kidding me? You're going to a meeting? I suppose saving my dad's life can just wait until you happen to have time to get around to it. Is that what you're saying? Well, my dad isn't sitting in some crappy jail because you're too busy staying here in your fancy office. You can just forget your meeting!" I'm shouting now. I know it. I just can't stop. "I am not leaving until you tell me how you're going to help my father." I plunk myself down on the blue leather chair. "He is not some client you can file away. He's my dad." I am shaking. I hope the lawyer can't see that. I fold my arms across my chest.

Mr. Baron picks up his phone and speaks into it. "Tell them it will be 15 minutes, set them up in the conference room, and take them some coffee, pastries, and my humble apologies." He puts the phone down.

"All right, Kevin. I wanted to try to figure out a way to soften this before I met with you, but you haven't given me time for that. I wanted time to try to change his mind about this, but you don't want to wait for that either. So listen carefully. I did go see your father yesterday. I asked him about you."

I interrupt. "Did you tell him I was here to see you? Did you tell him that I'm going to be helping you? Next time you go to see my dad, you can tell him that I'll be lining up all kinds of people who will swear that he could not possibly be the DB25 Monster! They'll swear he isn't that kind of a man." I can feel my hands gripping the arms of the chair so hard that they hurt.

"Son, maybe you better slow down a little. Against my advice, your father has instructed me to show this to you." The attorney opens a file drawer, withdraws a piece of paper, and hands it to me. I can hardly uncurl my fingers from the chair to take it.

It's in my dad's handwriting. "Kev, I'm so sorry. Yes, the good times we had were real. There's just a part of me that you can't—that you shouldn't even try to understand. There is only one thing that I can do for you now, and I am doing it. I will plead guilty. I will live with what I have done. Know that you could not have prevented any of this from happening. Know that you have done nothing wrong. This will be my last communication with you. I don't want you to attempt to contact me ever again. If you still want to do something for me, I ask you to forget that I ever existed—to live a life that wipes me from your memory. Be yourself, and be strong."

The letter is signed, and it looks like Dad's writing, and it doesn't sound like he's confused or has amnesia, but . . . but it can't be right. I stare at the attorney in disbelief. I gulp, "My dad isn't guilty. He told you that, right? So why would he even think of saying he was?"

Mr. Baron doesn't answer directly. "I always advise my clients to plead not guilty. It's up to the state to prove differently. That's what I have counseled your father as well. I also advised him that he shouldn't put anything in writing to anyone but me;

however, he insisted on your seeing this letter. "

"But why . . . why would Dad write this?" My eyes are burning, and my words come out kind of like a cry.

The lawyer shrugs. "I don't know. People can react very strangely to being in jail."

"But . . . but they don't plead guilty to terrible crimes they didn't commit! What did the DB25 killer do to my dad?"

Baron doesn't answer. He takes the letter from my hands and says that he'll keep it. "Obviously, we don't want something like this floating around, and you'll understand that, given Mr. Windor's wishes, it's probably best that you don't agitate him further."

Baron practically pats me on the head. "Just because Mr. Windor has written this letter doesn't mean we'll actually plead guilty. I'll do everything I can to put on the most vigorous defense that I can mount. If it helps, know that I win most of my cases. Now, please, let me work." He sends me on my way. I look back over my shoulder to see the lawyer heading down the plush green carpet toward some fancy conference room.

chapter 8

I FIND MYSELF IN THE stairwell of the lawyer's building, but I'm shaking too hard to walk down the steps. I sink down on a stair and put my head in my arms and let the sobs wrack my body.

Finally, I can cry no more. I make my way back to the bus stop. On the bus stop shelter billboard, there is an ad for McDonald's. A dad has his arm around his son, and they're walking into the restaurant after a ball game. I stare at that photo, and I think how many times that could have been my dad and me.

I am back on the bus. I know what I read in that lawyer's office, and the handwriting did look like my dad's. So what? Wasn't it Dad who taught me that you can't believe everything you read? Don't

I know my dad better than some piece of paper?

Maybe my dad's brain is so mixed up that he thinks he did it, or maybe he's been tortured. Well, the system may think they can do what they want because my dad has no one to stop it—no wife, no parents, no brothers or sisters. But my dad has me. If the police or the lawyers who are doing this to my dad think they can just write me off because I'm a kid, they're wrong. If they think getting my dad to write this letter will work, they're wrong again. One thing I know. I am my dad's best friend, and he is mine.

He would never ever ask me to abandon him as he has never abandoned me.

It's always been that way. I remember there was this one time when I was five. It was my weekend at Dad's, and he was inside and I was out in front. I saw a lost ball on the roof. I knew I shouldn't, but I climbed the trellis. The ball was stuck in the gutter. Grinning, I stuck my tongue through my two front missing teeth and proudly grabbed the stitching. Then with one hand holding the trellis and one clasping the ball, I started back down and lost my grip and slipped. I screamed. Somehow, my dad rushed out of the house, and he managed to catch me. Turned out I was fine, but Dad broke his arm. Makes no sense that he was able to catch me. How'd

he even know I was in trouble . . . he just did. That's
how it is between us.

When I get home, Mom's not there, and she won't be
back for another couple of hours. Do I tell her what
I did today? What the lawyer said? What I read?
What if she believes Dad's confession?

The phone starts ringing. It's got to be Mr. Baron.
He wants to tell me to come back. I'm so sure that I
don't even look at the caller ID. I grab the receiver
on the second ring.

"Thought you were coming to school today?" It's
Jason.

"Who is this?" I ask.

"Come on, you know who it is," Jason says.

He's right. I do know. We've been friends since
fourth-grade Little League. But I let the silence on
the phone linger. "So . . . uh . . . like I said . . .
thought you'd be back today," Jason finally says.

"I didn't make it."

"Yeah, well . . . I figured that out." Jason's voice
sounds strange; this conversation, if you can call it
that, is strange too.

More silence. "So, what do you want?" I ask.

"I . . . uh . . . I dunno. I mean, I guess, I just
wanted to say that I'm sorry."

"About . . ."

"Geez, about your dad. About the whole thing."

"Right. That would be why I've heard from you so many times since I got suspended. That would be why you have been around helping."

Jason sighs. "Sorry. I texted. You barely answered. I wanted to call . . . I didn't know what to say. I mean, I really thought your dad was a great guy too. I mean, no way you could have known . . ."

I cut him off. "There's nothing to know. My dad didn't do that stuff—not any of it."

"But they found him in that woman's . . ."

I cut Jason off. "And I'm telling you that my dad didn't do any of those things. You know my dad, so why don't you know better than to believe this crap in the media?"

"Okay . . ." Jason says.

"Not okay—not okay at all!" I shout into the phone. "When your dad didn't want you learning to drive a stick shift because it might mess up his precious sports car, who taught you how to drive? My dad."

There's silence. Then Jason says, "It'll be okay . . . they'll find out the reason your dad was in that apartment, and they'll let him go. Have you talked to him? Have you been to the jail to see him? Has he told you anything?"

"Why do you want to know?" I ask coldly.

"Hey, forget I said anything about it. Do you want to come to a pickup b-ball game after school tomorrow?"

A lot of things are going through my head. "You tell the other guys you're asking me?"

"Geez, Kevin, nobody gives a whole rundown of who's gonna come to a pickup game."

"Yeah," I say, "so why am I getting the special invite a day before a maybe game happens?

Again silence before Jason answers, "I don't know what to say that won't piss you off, so I'm gonna hang up. But I'm sorry about stuff . . . you know . . . and, Kev . . . why don't you come play b-ball tomorrow. I got a feeling you're gonna be great on offense."

Mom gets home from work late again today. She sinks onto a kitchen chair. "Do you care if we just heat up some soup tonight?"

"Okay, I'll do it," I say, opening up a couple of cans. Canned soup has pretty much been our dinner since Dad's arrest. Doesn't much matter since neither one of us is ever hungry now. Just another sign of change. Mom, who always relaxed by cooking and called herself the sovereign of soufflés and the princess of pies, now serves only canned soup and boxed crackers.

Mom takes a couple of sips of soup and pushes the bowl away. "So, how was school?" she asks wearily.

"Uh . . . school?"

Mom's voice takes on an edge. "Oh, Kevin, please, just tell me you didn't get in trouble again."

"Oh, great, go ahead . . . why not think the worst of your son?" I feel this unreasonable anger mounting. "Well, let's see . . . first I tried to blow up the stupid school, and then when that didn't work, I . . ."

Mom interrupts. "I'm sorry. Really. Let's start over. Tell me about your day."

Part of me says don't tell her anything. Let her think I went to school, and everything is okay. Part of me says that maybe she could help me, and she'll probably find out eventually anyway. While I'm trying to decide, Mom interprets my silence as that I'm still mad at her. She's not a great one for conflict. She says again, "I'm sorry." Then she adds, "I was thinking about you all day. I really want to know. How was school?"

"Well . . . uh . . . I didn't exactly go."

"You didn't go? You didn't go? You can't do this! You can't fail school now. We've got to hang on!" There's a slightly hysterical tone to her voice.

The phone interrupts with a shrill ring. I stand up to get it. "Wait," Moms calls, rushing over to check the caller ID. "I don't recognize that number. Don't answer." The phone continues to ring. Mom looks at me, runs a hand through her hair, and I swear there's gray there that didn't used to be. Neither of us speaks until finally the phone is silent. Then Mom picks up the conversation as if she had never stopped speaking. She pleads, "Kev . . . I . . . we just can't deal with anything else. You understand? I know it's easier to stay home, but please, you've got to go to school and do the things you used to do there."

I look at my mom—really look at her. She seems so fragile. The men of this family are taking their toll on her, so I don't tell her that I went to see Mr. Baron or what he said to me. I'll have to figure things out myself. I try to think of something to cheer her up— make her think things are normal. It's not that easy. Finally I say, "Hey, Jason called. He wants me to play in a basketball game after school tomorrow."

A tiny smile crosses Mom's lips. "I'm so glad," she says. "It'll be good for you to play basketball. You'll see. It'll help to be back in your normal routine."

"Yeah, I guess," I swirl my soupspoon around. "Mom, when you met Dad, what made you fall in love with him?" It just sort of pops out of my mouth.

"Oh, Kevin . . . let's not even think about going there. It's ancient history." Mom picks up the remote and turns the TV on. The screen is filled with Vanna and Pat and people guessing letters. Mom pretends to care about who wins.

Why should I be surprised at being shut out? When has Mom ever wanted to talk about Dad? She dabs her napkin at her eyes. Then she sees me staring at her. "Just tired, I guess," she says.

chapter 5

I **AWAKEN TODAY TO THE** smell of bacon cooking. Still half asleep, I wander into the kitchen thinking I might be dreaming. But no. It seems that Mom doesn't have to be at work early today, so she's decided to make me breakfast and drop me off at school. That's what she says. The real reason? I think maybe Mom wants to make sure I actually get to school today.

Our car ride is pretty weird. Guess maybe we're both thinking about our last time at school together with Mom taking me home looking like a punching bag. I see Mom gripping the wheel with both hands, and I think it'll actually be a relief when I can get out of the car. Funny thing though. When we get to Chapparal, and my eyes take in all the kids, my legs just don't seem to want to move. This could be harder than I thought.

Mom reaches over and squeezes my arm. "Kevin, you can do this. I know you can. Hold your head up high. Remember when you were a little boy; I used to tell you about how words could never hurt you? Every day will get a little easier. You've done nothing to be ashamed of."

I push the car door open. "And maybe Dad hasn't either." I slam it shut and don't look behind me. I don't know what's wrong with me. One minute I'm trying to protect my mom; the next I'm furious at her.

Big beige buildings loom in front of me. It seems surreal that I could have been going through these brown doors every day for the last three years without even thinking about it. Today, opening them feels like pushing 100-pound weights.

I feel almost as if I am watching myself. What would I think of me if I weren't me? Would I be looking at myself as a sort of strange freak? Would I be embarrassed to know me? Would I be disgusted? Hard to say.

I'm behind in every class. Guess maybe I should have spent some of that *Jerry Springer* time on the homework Mom worked so diligently to get, but I don't think I could have concentrated, even if I had wanted to.

Teachers' reactions to me vary. Leonard is a

straight-up guy. Tells me he's really glad I'm back, and not to worry about getting caught up, that it will all happen. I should give myself a little time. He has me stay after class and suggests I might want to talk to the social worker. I tell him I'm okay without that. Noyel is racing along in Spanish, doesn't even acknowledge that I was gone, but I must have missed a ton of vocabulary because I don't have a clue as to what she's saying. I notice I'm no longer sitting next to Emily. Seems while I was gone, Emily's seat changed for a guy in her place. Fine. If that's what she wants, she can have it just that way. I won't bother her ever again.

We're doing a lab in Chemistry. But McBee is a stickler that everything be done in order, so he says that I can't do this one until I've finished the two I missed last week. Suddenly, instead of my usual lab partner, I find myself assigned to work with Lani McQueen. Guess that's an indication of how low I've sunk. McBee says she's way behind too, but Lani is always way behind. She only drops into school occasionally, and when she does, she's always wearing her uniform of burgundy leggings and black clothes. Her hair is also black and burgundy, and as she reaches for a beaker, I notice that she's got every other fingernail painted black or burgundy too.

Lani transferred in last year. She showed up in my

History class second semester. Jacobson was so boring that jokes about Lani kept the class awake. Jerry Porfiro had new ones every day. It sort of made him famous. I don't remember most of them, but there was one about Lani walking into a bar that was pretty gross. I don't know. The jokes don't seem as funny now as they did then.

Jerry passed them around until one day, when Lani had actually shown up for class, somebody accidentally handed her the paper. Jacobson went right on with his boring lecture, but the whole class was focused on Lani. Jerry turned red. What was Lani going to do? She just folded the paper up into a small little square, stuck it into her mouth, and swallowed it. That really cemented her as a weirdo.

"Hey, you on drugs?" Lani is still holding the beaker. "I'm talking to you."

"I . . . uh . . . I guess I wasn't paying attention. What'd you say?"

Lani shakes her head, and the burgundy/black sways. So do the safety pins dangling from her ears. "Doesn't really matter, does it?" She fixes me with a look and puts the beaker down. "Welcome to the bottom of the high school feeding chain. I may even have to show up more this week to see how you do. A baby like you—you're gonna get eaten alive."

By the time the day is over, all I want to do is go

home. How did I ever like going to school here? On my way out, I feel my arm being grabbed. I tighten and get ready to fight. Then I hear Jason's voice.

"Hey, school's out—let's go play ball."

"I think I'll pass.

"Nope. No passes," Jason says, still gripping my arm "Come on, you got one day down. And it'll feel good to pound a ball through the hoop."

So mostly because I'm too tired to argue, I go. Jason talks as we walk. Something about his uncle knowing someone who might be able to get him a job as a water ski instructor at a sleep-away camp this summer. The words don't matter. Jason's using them to fill up nervous space, and I can almost hear his sigh of relief when we get to the park. Guys drift in. Usually, JL and Sam play, but I don't see them today. Don't know if that's because of me or because they just couldn't play.

"Okay," Jason says, "Listen up. I organized today's game, so I'm calling one captain. Who wants the other?"

Carl steps out and picks his first team member— Lance—at 6′ 6″, whenever he shows up to play, he usually gets picked first. He isn't that great, but it's tough to beat him down low. Then Jason takes me as his first pick. I'm embarrassed, but I feel good too. Jason's trying to make up for being a jerk last week.

Maybe I was too hard on him. I mean, I can't get my head around the whole Dad thing . . . maybe he can't either.

I stand next to Jason while he picks the rest of our team, and I figure I at least owe him trying to play a decent game. We flip to see who will be skins and who's shirts. We get skins, and we strip off our shirts. Their side definitely has height, but we're faster. It's a hard game. I let go of everything else, and my feet pound up and down the court. Jason's right. It feels good to concentrate on the ball and the net and nothing else. We win the first game and lose the second. It's starting to get dark, so we call this as last game. Sweat is pouring off me. My breath comes in ragged gasps . . . but I'm not the only one. Everyone starts trying trash talk to make up for rubbery legs and winded runs. Jason dribbles down court. I hear someone from the other team call, "Steal it! He holds the ball like a little baby." But Jason hangs on, passes, and then the ball is in my hands.

My defender gets in my face, tells me I'm too slow, too short, too freakin' spastic to make the shot count. My face contorts as I try to ignore him, concentrate, line it up, and shoot! The ball swooshes through the net. God, it feels good. Even though we end up losing the third game, it's only by a bucket, and we leave heads held high.

I walk home feeling both exhausted and elated. It feels like life is normal again. Okay. It's not that I really believe that. And it's not that I've abandoned my dad. It's just that normal feels so very, very great that I want to hang onto it for a little while longer.

At school, each day, I stay mostly to myself, but at least it seems like maybe the worst of the whispers are over. I guess people've decided this freak isn't doing anything all that interesting.

By Thursday, I'm still without a car. Jason'll take me to school, Mom'll drop me off, or I can always just jog. But I'd feel better to have my car back. What if it's just sitting in Dad's garage? Why am I so chicken to go see? I could at least check it out. When Mom gets home from work, I ask to borrow her car. She tells me it's low on gas.

"That's okay," I say.

"Where're you going?"

I shrug. "Just want to get out for a while."

"Uh . . . we could play Scrabble if you're bored."

"Yeah . . . well, actually, it's not so much about being bored as it is feeling kinda housebound with no wheels."

"Oh." Silence.

Mom really doesn't want me to take off in her car; these days, she only wants me at school or at home, either to protect me or to . . . but she can't think of a reason why I can't go out, so she hands me her keys.

In the midst of my relief, I look at her face and find myself promising her that I won't be gone that long. I put the car in gear and head toward Dad's. I won't even tell Mom I went to Dad's unless my Jeep is there, and I need her to drive me back to get it. I wonder if that yellow crime tape will be up. I wonder if there'll be police there. I wonder if they've trashed the place looking for . . . for who knows what.

I hope the reporters still aren't around. Maybe they never were. After all, nothing happened at Dad's condo, so why is my hand shaking on the gearshift when I turn down his street?

I don't know what I'm expecting, but when I get to Dad's, everything looks just like always. There's no yellow tape, no police, no reporters. I pull up on his driveway. Mom's car doesn't have the garage opener, so I get out and put my key in the front door. I keep expecting someone to jump out and stop me, but no one does. I let myself in Dad's house, wondering if the inside will be an awful mess. But the place looks the same. I swallow a big lump as I see two pairs of Dad's shoes still sitting on the floor by the sofa. It's . . . just like Dad should be home any second.

Until I get in his office. Dad's computer—gone. Dad's DVD collection—gone. All Dad's computer games—gone. Did the police take them? Did someone break in and steal them? Did Dad hide them? I look around for the little laptop that Dad had that last night I saw him, but it's gone too. The empty spaces stare at me, taunting me with no answers to anything.

It's so weird. I live here, but I feel like an intruder. I quickly head toward the garage, ready to check on the car, and get out. Please, car—be there! Be there! I silently urge. The garage is empty.

So that's it. I should just leave. But I don't. I feel zapped of everything. I sit in Dad's office, only without his computers, it doesn't even feel like Dad's.

As I sit there, I wish I had asked Dad a lot more questions instead of just playing games. Maybe, if I just knew more, I'd be able to figure things out better. But who's going to tell me details of Dad's life now? No one. I'll have to find answers myself. But how? I stare at Dad's desk. I can't believe I'm doing it, but I begin to open his desk drawers and file cabinets looking for some scrap of something that will explain anything. I tell myself it's nothing the cops haven't already done.

I try not to think about how much I'd hate anyone going through all my stuff. It's not that I have anything all that great; it's just that it's my private stuff. Still, maybe my dad left me some clue, something the police thought was useless, but I'd understand. That would make doing this okay, wouldn't it?

An hour later, I know that my dad's stuff only shows there is no secret side to him. I've violated his privacy for no reason. If there's some missing piece to the puzzle here, I'm too dumb to find it. If Dad left me some kind of clue, I didn't get it. I go back downstairs and lock the door to leave. Just as I'm pulling the key from the door, I hear, "Who's that? Who's there?"

I whirl around. It's Dad's next-door neighbor, old Mr. Seibert, standing on his front patio. "It's me . . . Kevin."

He peers at me through his Coke-bottle glasses and leans on his cane. "Say, you heard all that stuff they're saying about your dad?"

"Yes, but you know none of it is true," I say.

"I talked to a policeman or two and that reporter lady too. She came in my house, wired me up with the microphone and all, but I didn't see me on the TV news. Course I might have been sleeping when it was on."

"You . . . you talked to the police?"

Mr. Seibert nods. "Yep. There was a passel of them around here for a while. They started taking a

85

lot of stuff out of your dad's house. I asked them if they had a warrant. I know all about that from *Law & Order*. But they said they did. So I didn't try to stop them. I mean, what was I going to do? Call the police?" Mr. Siebert chuckles. "Get it . . . call the police . . . they were the police. They asked me a lot of questions."

"What . . . what kinds of questions were they asking you?"

Mr. Seibert shrugs. "I dunno. Too many to remember. But I told them your dad was a nice guy. I said I never seen him being violent or mad. I never seen him acting weird."

"Right," I say. "You're absolutely right." Finally, somebody who doesn't want to trash my father.

"Then I told those policemen I don't go butting into everybody's business, so how would I know what he did every minute."

My heart sinks. So much for a really positive endorsement of Dad.

Mr. Seibert shifts his cane. "I tell you, this street was a lot more crowded than I like with all those police and reporters. Too much confusion for me. I'm glad they finally all went away."

"Mr. Seibert, the one reporter . . . the one who interviewed you. You told her my dad wasn't guilty, right?"

"Hmm . . . well, yes, I think I did. I told her your dad helps me. That's it. That's what I said. I told her about how your dad set it up that the mower guy would mow my backyard too. Didn't even cost me any money. Since my hip, you know, I can't do it my-self anymore. I tell you, I hope your dad gets back pretty soon."

"Well, uh, Mr. Seibert, before the police and the reporters and stuff, did you ever see anyone else around here?"

"You mean like you?"

I try hard to keep my frustration in check. "Like anyone besides me who came around a lot?"

Mr. Seibert chuckles. "You sound just like those policemen."

I forge on. "When they asked you if you saw any-one else around here, what did you say?"

"I said no. I was plumb tired of answering so many questions. But there was your dad's friends, you know; they came a lot."

My heart started pounding. "I'm not sure who you mean . . ."

"Yeah, well maybe you weren't here so much when they came. I gotta go in. My hip is killing me."

"Wait. My dad's friends. Can you describe them?"

Mr. Seibert shook his head. "Macular degenera-tion."

"Huh?" I say.

"Macular degeneration. That's the name they call what's happening to my eyes. Peripheral vision is pretty good. Just can't quite make out things head on. But I know they were men and not ladies. I can still make that out! Well, I gotta go sit down. Nice seeing you, Kevin."

Mr. Seibert turned toward his door and slowly made his way into his house. "When you see your dad, you tell him for me that Alan Seibert hopes things work out better for him pretty soon. And if he did those awful things, it must be some other person living inside him he didn't even know about."

On the way home, I think about the friends that Mr. Seibert mentioned. Are they people who could help Dad? If they're really friends, how come I don't know about them? And then again, we're talking Mr. Seibert here. They could be the garbageman and FedEx guy.

When I pull into the driveway, I can see Mom's silhouette in the window. Guess she's been waiting and worrying. But when I get in the house, she pretends that she's barely noticed I was gone. So I pretend that I don't know she's upset that I left and didn't want to tell her where I was going. Maybe we're all a family of pretenders trying to be what we are not.

Did my parents only pretend to love each other? A long time ago, whenever I tried to ask about why they divorced, I just got the *it's a grown-up thing, but we both love you* crap. I let it go; maybe I believed that back then, or maybe it was hard enough to have Dad living somewhere else without asking questions no one wanted to answer. It was a long time ago.

Mom always has only spoken of dad in terms of "your father," but there must have been a lot more than that between them. They had to love each other enough to get married, didn't they?

I lie on my bed and toss a green Nerf ball up in the air. After Mom and Dad's split, I always thought it was kind of cool that Dad told me it was just me and him against the world. He had no other family. But what happened to his whole family? When I was about nine I asked Dad. He got real quiet, and then he said they were all dead. That seemed pretty sad, so I didn't say anything else. Then one time I asked Mom how they all died, and she looked surprised and told me I should talk with Dad about it. I wonder if divorced parents know how much their kids hate the ask-the-other-parent thing . . .

I hear the phone ring. Then Mom comes to my room. "Kevin, that was work. Jennie, one of my supervisors—well, her dad just died. She has to fly to Kansas on Saturday."

"Oh, that's too bad," I have no idea why my mother is telling me this.

"They want me to stay real late tomorrow so Jennie can show me how to do a new kind of database for a big new job before she leaves. It'll be overtime pay. But I'll say no if you'd like me to be here with you."

"Mom, I keep telling you, I don't need a babysitter. I'm fine. Really. Go."

I have to hear three choruses of "are you sure" before she leaves on Friday morning. I promise her that I'll be fine and head to school. When I get home, I think about hanging out here alone all night. It'll be okay. I could even catch up on some of my missing assignments. I get out my Chem book. It's the beginning of the weekend. I shut it again.

I think about calling Jason. At least stuff seems to be okay between us. We don't talk about any of the deep stuff, which is okay with me. I speed dial his number. "Hey, I got some great news for you!" I say.

"You grew 10 inches last night so at least you got height, since you don't got game," Jason says.

"Yeah, we both know my game would beat yours even if I shrank to only four feet."

Jason laughs, "So what's the great news?" he asks.

"Me." I reply.

"Trust me, you're never good news." Jason says.

"Yeah, you're probably right. In fact, I'll be bad news tonight at your house when you're the P-I-G in b-ball and toast in Xbox games, but hey, here's the good news. I'll still let you be my friend."

Jason doesn't answer, so I keep laying it on. "Leaves you speechless, huh? Can't even think of a comeback. That's okay. I don't mind being the friend who does it all better."

I'm on a roll. It feels great. I'm just gearing up for the best of the insults when Jason answers, "Uh, yeah, well, you're probably right."

Why's he throwing off our whole game? It's a rule. Neither of us ever gives in. Get zapped; try even harder to get the other one back. So what's up? Suddenly, I get it. He feels sorry for me. Don't kick the killer's son . . . he's already down. "Listen," I say, "No pity. Insult me just like always. Don't start apologizing ever! And when we play b-ball, you play me as hard as you can. I'll still beat you. And the same goes for video games or whatever else we do. Nobody cuts anybody any slack."

"Okay," Jason says.

"Okay," I say. "I mean it."

"Okay," Jason says again.

"Good," I say. "Then tonight, you want to find a

three-on-three for b-ball, or is it just me against you?

Jason says, "How about Saturday instead?"

"Alright," I say, "Tonight, I'll beat you one-on-one, and Saturday, I'll still let you be on my team for three-on-three."

Jason clears his throat. "Actually, tonight won't work."

"It won't?" Jason is always up for b-ball. "What else you going to do with Friday night? Tell me study, and I'll know that you're really an alien in Jason's place."

"Uh . . . well," Jason says.

Then I get it—it's Friday night—good old Jason's finally making a move! "You've actually got a date? Give it up. Who's the poor girl who took pity?" He doesn't answer. "Come on," I say. "It ain't gonna go away until I get the goods."

But Jason tells me that there's no date. He's just can't hang out tonight.

"Man . . . you that scared of my shot?" I taunt.

"Let's shoot hoops Saturday," Jason says. "I mean, don't you have homework and stuff that you need to get done tonight?"

"Uh, huh, nice try . . . you telling me about homework? Callie Alexander," I say triumphantly. "You're finally gonna make your move. About time. You've had a thing for her for long enough! Hey, I'm proud of you. I'll even go to Callie's with you—be your wing man. If it's good, I'm out of there. If you need help, I got your back, and if it's a disaster, at least I'll be around for b-ball. So . . . what time we going?"

"We're not," Jason says firmly.

"Fine, I'll just meet you there. Only, I don't remember where she lives. Fess up, buddy! "

"It isn't Callie."

"Yeah, right," I say. "I've seen you around the girl."

"That was a long time ago. I don't like Callie anymore."

"Okay, so if it isn't Callie—what's up tonight?"

Finally, Jason says that there is a party—at Emily's. I know I should, but I can't just shut up. "And . . ." I say roughly.

"And . . . I thought I'd go."

"And . . ." I let the word hang in the air.

"And you're not going to this party. It's no big deal," Jason says.

I don't know what's wrong with me. I know Emily doesn't want me around, but I keep at it—keep saying that I'm coming to the party until Jason finally has to say that Emily has warned him her parents will call the police and have me arrested for trespassing if I show up on their property. He says her parents are just stupid. Emily can't help it. "So, we'll hang on Saturday, right?"

"Yeah . . . no, I don't think so."

"Ah, come on—don't turn this into a big deal," Jason says.

"I'm not. You're the one making a big deal about tomorrow."

"Okay," Jason says, sounding ticked off. "Then nobody's making a big deal about anything. I'll see you Monday." The line goes dead.

I slam the phone down. It's not fair. It's not supposed to be everyone except Kevin. Why won't Emily stand up to her parents and tell them I've always been a great guy to her? Why won't Jason refuse to go to their stinking party if they won't have me there? God, I feel so totally alone. Dad—what have you done?

On Friday night I actually think about getting dressed and showing up at Emily's uninvited. I'll confront her parents. I'll call them out for the hypocrites they are. I'll make them apologize. No way they should be treating me this way. No way.

I'm actually starting in for the shower when I give myself a little reality check. What if they mean it, and they do call the cops? It is their property. I'd be trespassing. The cops could arrest me. Wouldn't the media just love that? They could run Dad's and my mug shots side by side.

So I stay home. But my mind is centered on that party all night. Who's there? What are they doing? Is Emily hanging out with some other guy saying how much fun she's having?

I fall asleep hoping that she had a miserable time. I hope Jason got totally shut down playing basketball there. In fact, I hope the whole night bombed so much for everyone that no one will want to party at Emily's ever again.

I awaken to hear Mom getting ready to go out for her morning jog, and suddenly, I feel this surging gratefulness for her. We may never understand each other, but I can count on the routineness of her life. She goes to work at the same place for eight hours a day, and then she's home. Mom would never end up getting arrested in someone's apartment bathroom.

On the spur of the moment, I hurry over to Starbucks while she's gone and get her a mocha Frappuccino. It's her favorite, but she says they're too expensive—so she always drinks the plain stuff she brews at home.

I know I don't have the money for my daily Starbucks fix anymore either, but I figure my mom and I could both use a break. As I get back to the house with two mocha Frappuccinos, I can hear the shower. She's already back from her run, thinking I'm still my usual asleep until Saturday noon. When she walks into the kitchen, I'm sitting at the table. "Brought you something." I hold up the cup of frothy coffee.

"Oh, my. Oh, thanks," she says. "How sweet!" She swirls the straw and takes a deep sip. "Uhmm, delicious!" Her eyes well up with tears. "You are such a great son."

Now I'm embarrassed. "Mom, it's just a cup of coffee." I slurp some whipped cream off the top of my drink. "So how was work?"

She shrugs. "Work is work. Jennie explained about the price changes that had to be entered before the sale, not too exciting, but extra money for us." I think about my mom being a data processor. Me or Dad, we'd lose our minds in a job like that, but Mom doesn't seem to care.

Things are nice sitting here this morning. I feel good about what I did getting the coffee, so I don't know why I have to spoil it. Still, I open my mouth. "Mom, I have some questions about Dad."

She seems to almost shrink into herself. There's no response. "Mom," I say. "Please. Maybe you can't make this whole arrest thing go away, and it's certainly not your fault, but please talk to me. There's so much I don't know."

She's silent for a minute more, and then in a soft

voice she says, "Kevin, I don't know what secrets you think I have, but I am at a complete loss as to how your father could possibly be the DB25 Monster. You probably know your dad better than anyone, so either this whole thing is a terrible mix-up or maybe—no one really knows him at all."

"Mom!"

Mom sighs. "Kevin, can't we just drop this? I don't see what it . . ."

I interrupt. "We can't drop it! I need to know why or how Dad could have been in that woman's bathroom. You're the only one who can give me pieces of his life that . . ."

"I don't have any pieces that could help you. Really." Mom starts to get up from the table, the rest of her Frappuccino now untouched. "I have laundry . . ."

I yell at her. "Look at this face. It's my father's face. You can rebuild your life, be someone else, but I will always be my father's son."

chapter 10

SO I'D LIKE TO SAY that this dramatic moment suddenly unleashes a torrent of truth, but all that happens is that Mom tells me that yes, I will always be my father's son. I will always be her son as well. But most of all, I will be myself. And I'm a wonderful person with nothing to apologize for, ever.

I try to get her to talk more, to finally tell me what happened between her and Dad, but despite all my prodding, the only thing she'll say is, "He broke my heart. But it was a very long time ago, and he gave me you, so it was worth it." Then she leaves to sort the whites from the colors.

I try doing some Pre-Cal, but it makes no sense. Great, I'm going to have to go in for extra help. I head outside to shoot hoops. Maybe I'll call Jason, tell him I changed my mind about hanging out tonight. We can play ball. We don't have to talk about Emily's party. All I want to know is if she was with someone. Maybe she was miserable too. Maybe it's just that her stupid parents were being impossible. I bang the ball against the board.

I flip open my cell to call Jason a couple times, then decide maybe I'll just text instead. But I don't do either. I know that if I'd been the one there and he was home, I'd have sent a text from the party saying it was lame, and he was missing nothing.

I walk back into the house to get a drink, and I see Mom's discarded Frappuccino sitting in the sink. I think about her smile as I handed it to her. Actually, I guess she doesn't smile all that often. And really, why should she? She works at a low-paying, lousy job to pay her share of things. When was the last time Mom was out doing anything fun? Mid-afternoon, I stick my head in the kitchen doorway. "Tell you what, Mom. Why don't we go to a movie tonight?"

She sets the iron down. "We . . . who?"

Okay, so I haven't asked my mom to do anything special since . . . well, I can't really remember when. But in my defense, what teenager hangs out with his parent on a Saturday night? And besides, I spend a lot of weekends at Dad's. "We . . . you and me. I'll even treat if we go to the cheap movie theater."

Mom smiles, comes over, and ruffles my hair. She used to have to lean down to do that. Now, she has to reach up. "It's okay, Kevin. We're going to be okay."

As she tries to comfort me, I feel suddenly protective, "Sure we are. But about the movie . . . what do you say? Imagine what it would do to a guy's self-esteem if his own mom turned him down for a movie."

Mom sighs, "Can I take a raincheck?"

"You're turning me down?" I say in disbelief.

Mom explains, "Never! But Linda Arongilly—our neighbor from the old apartment—called to say she's in town. I invited her over for tonight. I'd cancel, but she was my dearest friend years ago, and it's been so long. She's leaving tomorrow, and I'd really like to see her. Do you remember Linda at all?"

I shake my head no. Mom offers, "Why don't I call Linda and tell her we're all going to have dinner together and maybe see a movie? It would be fun."

I bow out of that one real fast. The day slides by. I don't call Jason. He doesn't call me. At about 6:00, I hear our doorbell, and then wisps of chatter from the living room. I have no desire to get reintroduced to this Linda and hear how I've grown . . . duh . . . what kid hasn't between 7 and 17? So the plan is to hide out in my room, but I get hungry. Mom snags me as I head toward the kitchen. Linda is holding a mug of coffee. She takes one look at me, gasps, and drops her coffee. She's all over herself apologizing, and she says to Mom, "I'm just sooo sorry, but my God, he's the carbon copy of Greg. He just scared . . . I mean . . . he just . . . I just didn't expect . . ." She's stops speaking and keeps mopping the coffee. "If you've got a little club soda, I can get the coffee out before it stains."

I'm not sure where I'm going, but I'm getting out of this house. I throw on a jacket and leave. I start jogging either to warm up or to run away from my world or both. I don't know how far I've run, when I hear, "Well, it's nice you showed up even if you are late."

"Huh?" I say, stopping. It's dark out, and all I can tell is the voice is coming from a girl who's smoking a cigarette. "Uh . . . I think you have the wrong person."

"Kevin Windor."

"Yeah . . ." I squint into the darkness, but all I can see clearly is the red glow of the cigarette tip. "And you would be . . ."

"How quickly they want to forget when they've been sent to Loserville in Chemistry."

"Lani?"

"Here and in person."

"Because . . ."

She sighs, "Because I live around here . . . at least for this month. Group home over there. No smoking allowed inside."

"What kind of group home?" I ask.

"Aren't you the nosy one," she says. "What're you doing in my neighborhood?"

I change the subject. "How do you expect to pass Chemistry if you never show up?"

She puffs on her cigarette. "I don't."

"Then why show up at all?"

Lani moves over into the shadows of the streetlight. She stubs out her cigarette, takes another one, and lights it. "I get bored."

After my enforced confinement at home, I can almost understand what she means. "Yeah, well you're gonna get dead pretty soon if you keep sucking down those things."

Lani laughs, "How sweet. I didn't know you cared."

It's too weird that I'm standing here talking to Lani. I mean, I've barely said two words to her since she's been at Chapparal. She's just not my kind of girl. My kind of girl—Emily's heart-shaped face and sparkling blue eyes pop unbidden into my brain.

"Hey, want to see my new piercing?"

"Huh?" I say.

"Yeah, it's okay. I'm used to people not listening. See ya in Chemistry—if I show up, that is."

"Wait." I can't believe I'm saying it. But I don't want to go home. I don't want to head over to Jason's, and I'm tired of being alone. So Lani and I sit down on the curb. It's like people from two different planets having a conversation. But only for a while. We find out that we both like that old group the Bee Gees, which is weird because they were famous from like before we were even born.

Lani does a great imitation of "Stayin' Alive" that cracks us both up. We talk about Travolta in his white suit dancing to the song in the movie *Saturday Night Fever*. I can't believe she knows all about it. I think the movie's hilarious, but when I showed the DVD to my friends, they said it tanked and turned it off after five minutes. Lani and I talk about the movie and then move on to other movies and music we like. She seems pretty normal tonight, and I wonder what it must be like to live with a group instead of parents. I motion in the direction of the group home. "Is it hard to live there?"

She shrugs. "Better than my mom's or the seven foster families after her."

"You left because you and your mom couldn't get along?"

Lani laughs. "Not exactly, choirboy. I was six."

"I'm sorry." I don't know exactly what else to say. I can't imagine getting yanked out of your house at six years old.

Lani lights up still another cigarette, takes a drag, and blows a smoke ring. We watch it dissolve in the air. Then she shrugs, "Forget the sorry. It's all ancient history."

"Did . . . did you know you were going to have to leave?"

Lani blows another smoke ring. "Nope. Cops came to my house, looked around, and took me away. Next thing I knew, I got sent to live with my first foster family. That didn't work out. So they put me in another one; it was worse. You ever tried getting along in some foster familes?"

"Nope. I've got enough problems with my real family." I can't believe that popped out of my mouth.

Lani grins. "Yeah, I bet you do. But they don't put you in foster for that."

I'm afraid to trust what I might say, so I keep my mouth shut. Lani doesn't seem to notice. She continues talking. "I like this group home well enough. It's better than my fosters, except I can't smoke here, and some of my housemates are a little bizarro."

For Lani to think people are bizarre . . . I can't even imagine what they must look like. But it sounds like she's had a pretty crummy life. The kids at school probably haven't helped. Maybe they wouldn't give her such a hard time if she didn't look so weird. Maybe that stuff was okay at other schools, but it doesn't work here.

"Hey, can I ask you something?"

"Sure." She stubs out her cigarette. "No guarantees I'll answer."

"Okay, what's with your clothes and your multicolored hair, and all the safety pins hanging from your ears?"

She tells me if I'm too dumb to figure it out, it doesn't matter. "In fact, you're not too smart about other stuff either."

"Such as . . ."

"Such as your dad. You're not the first one to have screwed-up parents. It's not your fault, but you're going to pay and pay and pay for his mistakes if you care. Blow the whole thing off. And quit trying to make sense of it all. Crappy parents will never make any sense."

"But my dad isn't crappy, and he isn't guilty."

"Right. That's what they all say. Look, your dad might have made a bigger splash than most, but you're not all that special."

I look at Lani. "Do you . . . do you know people in prison?"

She laughs. "God, are you some kind of Boy Scout? You need to grow up."

"I am grown up," I say defensively. "And you . . ." I stop what I was going to say. It just doesn't seem so fun to be mean to her with her life like it is. "Lani, do you ever think about your mom?" I ask.

"My mom is off-limits to you, little Scout." Then she yawns and says she's going in.

I walk back to my house, but I've already decided that if Linda's car is still parked in front, I'm going to sneak in the back way. Maybe I should stay away regardless. If some woman who hasn't even seen me in ten years is repulsed, what must living with my face every day be doing to my mom?

But it's cold and I'm tired, really tired. I quietly let myself in the back way. If Mom and Linda are still in the living room, I should be able to sneak into my room with no one being the wiser. Then a floorboard squeaks. I stand frozen to the spot until the noise is absorbed. And while I'm waiting to move, I can hear them. They're talking about Dad!

I stand in the dark, letting the conversation wash over me. Linda says, "Even before, I didn't have much use for your ex. He and his own father deserve each other. Do you know if they ever made up?"

Then Mom's voice. "Well, Kevin has never met his

grandfather. So I'd have to say they never reconciled."

A grandfather! I don't know what to think. Dad said his parents were dead. Why don't I know anything about this family!

I creep down the hallway until I'm right outside the living room. If one of them leaves to use the bathroom, there's no way I can move fast enough not to be discovered. But I have to take the chance. Finally, maybe I'll find out about my dad's past. I'm so close that I can even hear the spoon clinking as Linda stirs her coffee.

Mom's voice: "I'm so glad you're here. It feels so good to talk to someone. And there're so many things I don't have to explain to you."

Linda's voice again: "I was horrified when I saw Greg's mug shot on TV. I can't even imagine how it must have been for you."

Mom: "It's been pretty horrible."

Linda: "I'm so sorry. I can't believe even after all this time, he keeps causing you pain. Do you think they'll find him guilty?"

I'm holding my breath, and not just because I'm worried about being discovered. There's silence for a minute before Mom speaks. "I think about Kevin, and what a great kid he is. And Kevin and Greg have always been so close, so this man my son loves so much, he couldn't be a monster. But then . . . then I think about the other side of Greg—my begging him to stay. I think about how much I loved him . . . and . . ."

"Here. Here's a tissue," Linda says.

Mom's voice is jagged now. "I can still see it all so clearly. Greg had finally graduated from college. It had been so tough, and it took so long, but he'd done it. I'd even splurged on a special dinner to celebrate. But Greg . . . he came home that night, blew out the candles, turned on the overhead light, and told me that he just couldn't do it anymore. We were both still young enough to lead our own lives, and it was time for us to do so. You know, he actually reached over and shook my hand. He wished me a nice life, told me he'd take care of Kevin financially, and then walked out of my world. Just like that. It didn't matter that I begged him, pleaded with him, told him he was the love of my life. He listened politely like I was telling him about a grocery list. So, even when he was my husband, I must not have known him at all. And now, how can I possibly know who or what he is?"

The words hang in the air until Linda picks up the conversation. "His whole family treated you like dirt."

Mom's voice: "It was pretty awful, but to be fair,

it wasn't just me. They were awful to Greg too." She sighs. "Ancient history now. Honestly, I try not to think too much about it . . . it just upsets me all over again." Deep sigh. "So do you think you'll stay in Denver?"

Mom and Linda start talking about Denver and Linda's job there, and I stumble outside to try to clear my head. So Dad and Mom. They didn't *both* decide that divorce was best for everyone? And Dad's family—his parents weren't dead after all?

I sit down on the driveway trying to make sense out of everything. I have to take charge, to get a handle on my own life. I am going to confront Mom tonight, and I won't give up until I get the truth. I'll just wait until Linda leaves, and then Mom will have to talk to me; I won't let it drop. She has to tell me. She owes me at least that!

I'm pacing the driveway still trying to figure it all out when Linda comes out the door. She doesn't look any happier to run into me than I am to see her. In fact, she jumps a little. "What . . . what're you doing out here?"

"I'd like to talk to you before you go."

Linda takes a deep breath, glances around our empty street, and keeps walking. "Sorry. I really don't have time tonight."

Her car is parked a little way down, and I tell her

that I'll walk her to it. "It's . . . it's okay. You can go back inside now."

I keep walking right next to her. "Tell me about my parents."

She ignores me, opens her car door, and it looks like she's going to swing it shut and take off before she says a word to me. I can't let her leave. I jump into her backseat. "I'm not getting out of this car until I get answers to my questions."

Linda looks in the rearview mirror and gasps. She opens her car door, probably to march back into the house and tell my mom that her son is a lunatic. I can't let her do that. Mom's got enough on her plate and sure doesn't need me causing her any more trouble.

"Wait. Please. I just want to know about my parents. I can't ask my dad now, and my mom never wants to talk about it."

"Then I have nothing to say to you either. Now, get out of my car." Linda commands.

I push open the back door and leave. I start to apologize again. But Linda guns her motor, and I watch the car roar off into the night. I put my hands over my head. What in the hell is the matter with me?

I sit outside for a long time. Who am I? I do not force my way into women's cars . . . I am not that kind of person . . . so who did that tonight?

Finally, I drag myself inside, climb into bed, and fall into a dreamless sleep. In the morning I wonder if I dreamed the whole thing. When I get down to the kitchen, Mom is sitting having coffee. She's already been for her run and showered and dressed. She's smiling. "Good morning, my night-owl son! I tried to wait up for you, but I fell asleep. I wish you'd stayed around for a while last night. You'd have really liked Linda if you'd gotten to know her. She was such a dear friend of mine. We had such a lovely visit."

"Well . . . uh . . . I'm glad you had a good time," I mumble.

But Mom doesn't seem to notice that anything's wrong with me. She rarely chatters, but she's going on about Linda and how great her friend looks and how she wishes Linda wasn't leaving town today. "I offered to take her to the airport, but she said the Marriott shuttle goes there for free, and I shouldn't bother," Mom says.

Well, that's good. Maybe Linda won't talk to Mom before she leaves. Maybe she won't tell Mom that I'm some kind of pervert if I can explain first.

I excuse myself, go to my room, and call the Marriott on my cell phone. When Linda finds out it's me, I'm sure she'll hang up, so when I hear the hello, I try to get everything out without even taking a breath. "I'm calling to say I'm so sorry about last night—I just needed to find out about my mom and dad and my mom will never talk about them—And now with things with my dad—I'm so confused— you're the only person I've found who could give me answers—I didn't mean to scare you—I just wanted you to talk to me." Finally, I have to stop. I have to breathe. I'm pretty sure that I'm going to be hearing the sound of the dial tone in my ear, but at least I tried.

Linda is still on the phone! She says, "Your mother is one of the dearest people in the world, and she's gotten a lot of really rotten breaks in life. If she doesn't want to discuss your father, she shouldn't have to. I'll tell you what I know so you'll leave her alone about it. But then I don't want you to bother me again."

I promise, and Linda begins speaking. She explains that she knows the early part of Mom and Dad to- gether only from what Mom told her. Linda says, "Your parents met when your mom was only 15. She'd just moved to Boise because her grandmother had taken custody of her. Your mom never said what happened to her own mother. I think it was a tough move for her, but it got a lot better when your dad was assigned to show the new transfer student around.

Your mom said that without having been assigned to be her guide, your dad would never have noticed her. She said he was Boise High's smartest kid ever, and one of the most popular.

Linda continues, "I think your mom just didn't have confidence in herself. She's pretty enough. That's what I've told her. Anyway, your folks became a couple. Your dad liked your mom so much that he decided he'd go to the University of Idaho instead of Yale so they'd still be near each other.

Linda continues, "That made your grandfather furious, and he forbade your dad to ever see your mom again. But they were sure they were in love and destined to be together."

"It's hard to imagine them young," I say.

"Your mother was sixteen." Linda says. "Which was the reason they sneaked off to Georgia, where it was legal to marry. But your mom was afraid that your grandfather would still separate them, so they stayed there long enough to make sure your mother was pregnant with you. Then they went home. They actually thought your father could return, still be the valedictorian, and since they were married, your dad could take her with him to Yale."

"But it didn't happen that way," I say softly.

"No." Linda says, "It didn't. Your grandfather was so mad at your dad that he disowned him and told him to live with the trash he'd dragged in. Your dad dropped out of all his smart-kid classes and got a job in the back of some computer store working repairs. Your mom quit school and got a job as a waitress until you were born. Then soon as your father got his diploma, they left Boise."

My head's reeling. Linda continues. She met Mom and Dad when they moved into a tiny rental place over a garage of the house next door to her. They had zero money, and Mom was home alone with me. Dad would work all day and then go to school at night. Because Mom didn't even have her high school diploma, child care would have cost more than she could have made working, so she stayed home with me. Linda said she felt sorry for Mom, who was always alone without even a car. So that's why she first invited Mom over for coffee.

She was so excited for Mom when Dad finally graduated from college. Even though she'd miss having Mom next door, life was finally going to be easier for them. They could even afford a real place to live. "Your mom was so thrilled—except, just then, your father announced that he was leaving her."

I interrupt. "That's not like my father."

Linda's voice is cold and sarcastic. "Right, he's

such a prince of a man. Look, your mom deserves a lot better than life's given her. I don't think she can take much more, so why don't you work hard on being a decent son."

The phone line goes dead.

chapter 11

I VOW THAT I WILL try to be nicer to my mom. On Sunday, I volunteer to trim the overgrown hedge in the front yard. Mom is very appreciative. She doesn't even mention that she first asked me to do it almost six months ago. The thing is such a mess that it takes most of the afternoon. When I'm finally done, I sink on the sofa to watch an old movie. I guess I must have fallen asleep because suddenly it's dark out, meaning it's Sunday night—a homework procrastinator's purgatory. And right now I'm there big time. Wish I could hire someone to do some makeup work for me. Then I could sit back, watch TV, snack on chips and salsa, and call, "How's it coming? I need it all caught up by tomorrow!" Nice fantasy. Even if I could find such a person, they'd want money . . . and I happen not to have any.

Dad always said, "Your job is school. Get the grades and the rest is up to me."

How easily I just accepted that the generous allowance would always be available. I turn on the computer thinking I should get a job; I find out fast that I don't qualify for any of the even marginally interesting ones.

I wonder how much Dad makes? He always seemed to have a lot of money. But then computer geeks can charge a lot, I guess. We never talked about it. Now, I have a million questions for him and no way to get any answers.

The cursor on the computer blinks at me: I stare. I start the business letter for English; I wish I were writing to Dad instead. And suddenly, I stop. So why can't I? I'll write to my dad and mail the letter to Mr. Baron. He'll give it to Dad, and then Dad will want to see me. I'll go to that jail, and together, Dad and me, we'll get things straightened out.

"Dear Dad," I type. Then I stop. What if something I write gets twisted and causes trouble for Dad? I tell myself I'm being paranoid. I've watched too much *Law & Order* on TV. But then again, my dad is in jail . . . real jail . . . accused of crimes that are even worse than anything on *Law & Order*. Finally, I just write, "I want to see you and talk to you more than anything. (Yeah, I want it even more than the red Ferrari.)" I think maybe that will make him smile, and at least he'll know for sure it's me. I smile myself remembering all the times Dad and I visited "my" Ferrari at Spinakers Fine Autos.

But I'm not at any auto dealer's, and I'm not with my dad. I look at the waiting computer screen, and my fingers type, "Please, please, please, just let me come see you. I promise after I've come once, I won't ever bother you if you don't want to see me again."

I wish I'd written this letter sooner. I should have done it right away. I know that after Dad reads this, he'll have his lawyer call me. It might be a little weird to go into a jail, but I'll handle it. I mean, Dad's had to endure it for weeks now. Wish I knew someone who'd been to visit in jail so I could kind of find out what's the right thing to do. Maybe I'll let Mr. Baron come with me the first time.

The phone starts ringing. To please Mom, I look over at the caller ID before answering. It's Jason. Should I answer? I'm really pissed at him for going to the party, but he's about the only one who's at least tried to stick by me. Besides, he might be calling to say he's sorry, and the party was totally lame.

So I'll answer, but I'll let him sweat. Let him keep apologizing! If the situation had been reversed, I would've skipped the party and played b-ball with

Jason. Well, at least I think that's what I would have done.

I pick up the receiver. "Hey . . ." comes Jason's voice from the other end. "Thought you might like a break from writing your Government paper."

"Haven't started it yet," I reply.

"Yeah, me either," Jason says. "Sunday nights are supposed to be spent sitting in front of the tube, relaxing after a great weekend. There ought to be laws that teachers can't assign homework over weekends."

"At least your paper only has to be three pages," I remind him.

"Yeah, Mr. AP guy. I told you it's dumb to think you're so smart," he says. "What've you got to do, ten pages?"

"Eight," I admit. I wait for Jason to bring up the party, but he doesn't. Finally, I tell him, "I gotta get started on my paper. It's not worth an all-nighter." I start to hang up, but he keeps talking. He goes off about some basketball trade that might happen between Denver and Phoenix. Finally, I tell him that unless he wants to write both our papers, I'm hanging up.

"Yeah . . . well, there's one more thing." He says. I wait. There's silence.

"Well, what?" I ask.

Jason sighs. "Well . . . I don't . . . it's just that I don't want you to go to school tomorrow and hear this from somebody else."

I can feel a funny taste in my mouth. I want to hang up right now before Jason can say one more word, but he blurts out, "I kind of hooked up with Emily Friday night. I didn't plan to or anything."

"My Emily?" I feel like I'm choking.

"Hey . . . come on! She's not *your* Emily. Geez, Kev . . . face it! She never was."

I don't say one word. I can feel my fingers gripping the phone tightly. Jason continues. "Look, I know you liked her, so I'm sorry. You know I would've never hit on her, but now, she's made it real clear she's never gonna be your Emily. So, when her and me, we sort of really got along, it wasn't like I was taking her away from you, right?"

I don't answer. Jason says, "Come on, you gotta admit that."

I am still not saying anything. I sit down on my bed. If I could make my fingers let go of the phone, I'd hang up. But Jason drones on, "Hey, I wish you'd talk."

Silence. I can hear myself breathing. "Well, anyway, I didn't want you to think I just did it to piss you off or anything. It wasn't like that." I still don't say anything. Jason goes on, "So . . . me and you are good, right? Okay, then."

"No, we're not good." I shout into the phone. "You're a lousy jerk and a poor excuse for a friend." I'm glad I've said it. It feels good to let him know how things stand. It would feel even better if I hadn't waited until after Jason had hung up.

Today, I pack a PB&J sandwich. No way I'm going in the cafeteria and sitting next to Jason pretending that everything is just fine. The rules are that you don't hit on your friend's girl. Period. No exceptions.

On my way to school, I stop at the mailbox to deposit my letter to Dad. I wish I could take it to Baron in person, but I've got no car, and I've promised Mom no more missing school. I open the mailbox handle. My hand is shaking. Please, please let this work, I think. The letter slides into the box. I stare at it, unable to move for a minute. Then I turn toward school. I can get there on time if I jog at a good pace, but it'd be so much better to have my car. I feel like an underclassman. Even if the police took my car, Dad's car might still be at the repair shop. I pull out my cell and get the number from information. The service department there assures me that Dad's car has not been in the shop for four months. I hang up and for one crazy second, I wonder if Dad's supposedly "being repaired" car is actually sitting at the crime scene undiscovered.

What kind of son thinks such things? I'm so ashamed! I wipe the thought from my mind.

In third hour, Mrs. M. is droning about a semicircle with a rectangle in it where the radius of the semicircle is 10, and we're supposed to find a function that models the area A of the rectangle in terms of its height H. No one really cares about the As and the Hs. Only Mrs. M. can get all worked up about Pre-Cal. We've joked that her whole house is probably wallpapered in white boards so she can do calculus problems anywhere.

The door to the classroom opens, and Mrs. M. glowers at the office messenger who has dared to interrupt her class. The messenger hands her a note and beats it out of the room fast. Mrs. M. is legendary on campus for not liking any intruders, as she calls them, during her teaching. She has to adjust the glasses on her nose to read the note. "Kevin," she says, frowning at me, as if I caused the messenger to interrupt, "Go to the office."

I pick up my backpack and stand up, taking the note from Mrs. M.'s outstretched hand. I see Crystal lean over to whisper something to Daniel and point to me. He shakes his head. I look down at the note. I have been summoned to the social worker.

No one in my group of friends has ever been to see the social worker. Until all this happened, I didn't even know our school had one. I've told everyone who asked that I didn't need to see her. Obviously, no one was listening. I already know she'll have nothing to say once I get there. She can't change all the stuff that's happening. So what can she do to help? And if people find out that I'm seeing a social worker, it'll be one more thing to add to my being a freak. I'm going to make it clear that I don't want her to bother me again, not tomorrow, not next week, not EVER again. However, when I get to her office, the door is closed. I try the knob. It's locked. I knock gently. A voice says, "I'm just finishing up with another situation. I'll be with you in a few minutes. Go ahead and have a seat in the main office waiting area."

I head back for the green upholstered chairs in the main lobby wondering if that's what I am too—a situation. I sure hope no one walks in and asks me what I'm waiting for. Finally, the social worker calls me in. She asks how I'm doing. I tell her that I'm okay. She asks me about some longer-term counseling. Have I talked with my mom about it? I tell her that I won't need it. After my dad's freed, I'll just need apologies from all the people who falsely accused him.

The social worker makes some notes on a sheet in front of her. I can see her black fountain pen delivering ink onto the page and hear the scratchings the nib makes, but I can't see what she's writing.

At last, she puts her pen down and looks at me. I look back and say, "Please do not call me up to this office again."

"I don't think the office is the problem. I wish you would let me help you, but I can't do that unless you help me know your concerns and needs."

"What I need is for you to leave me alone. What concerns me is coming to your office when I don't need to."

The social worker sighs and runs her hand lightly across a large stack of folders. She says, "Well, if you change your mind, you know you're always welcome."

"Okay." I guess now she can mark me off on some chart to show she's doing her job. I get my backpack; I'm ready to escape. Then I surprise myself by stopping and asking, "You ever go see someone in jail?"

Her eyes widen. "Uh, no, no I haven't."

"Yeah, well, okay, then, forget it."

"Wait, Kevin. I have a pamphlet all about jail visitation. I'll just look for it." She opens a big file cabinet and mutters, "Now where did I put all those brochures from the state . . . they must be here somewhere."

I open the door to her office. "Never mind." I wonder briefly if it's a statement of how important she is in this school that she's got the smallest of all the offices. The college counselor's is twice as big. I guess that's because at our school, there are a lot more kids trying to decide whether college A or B is better for them than figuring out whether or not their parents are killers.

The bell's going to ring pretty soon, so I decide I'll just take an early lunch even though I'm not very hungry. I know I probably should head back for whatever Pre-Cal explanation is left. I definitely didn't get my Dad's math genes. He'd already finished Calculus and some community college probability seminar by my age. I used to think our math skills were almost the only way the two of us weren't exactly alike.

chapter 12

TWO DAYS PASS. I'VE checked my cell phone a hundred times. I've checked the house phone just as many. No call from the lawyer. No return call from the message I left with his receptionist. I should have gone down in person. I should have shoved that letter in Mr. Baron's face and told him I wanted it taken to my dad right then. All my life, I've been the "good kid." Listen to authority. Give in. Don't make waves. Plain old passive Kevin. Well, no more.

Today, I get home from school and see there are still no messages on the answering machine. That's it. I'm going down to Mr. Baron's right now and giving the guy a piece of my mind. His fancy office won't stop me. I'm almost out the door when I happen to glance at the clock.

There's no way I can take the bus and get clear to

Baron's office before the place closes. I pick up the phone. If the receptionist says Baron's too busy to talk to me, I'll just tell her that I'm tying up the line until he isn't too busy to talk to me, and I don't care if that's the rest of the afternoon. Let's see how fast that lawyer can find his way to the phone after that. And while I've got him on the phone, I'm going to find out about my car.

If Mr. Rodney Baron hasn't already done it, he's going to jail tomorrow morning to give my dad my letter. I'll go too. That way, I can make sure it'll happen, and I'll finally see my dad.

I dial. A female voice answers with the twenty names of the law firm again. I take a deep breath. "I'd like to speak with . . ." My voice cracks like I was 12 or something. "Mr. Rodney Baron."

The voice replies, "And whom shall I say is calling?"

I sigh deeply. We've already done this drill. "I'm Kevin Windor, Greg Windor's son. I think we may have met when I was in the office."

Her voice changes slightly as she says, "Oh, yes. Uhhhm . . . Mr. Baron is out of the office."

I can feel my temper starting. "Really? Then why didn't you say so until *after* you knew who was calling? You can just tell Mr. Baron that I'm not hanging up until he's suddenly back *in* the office."

"No, really," the receptionist sounds a little breath-less. "He's really out of the office. We're just always supposed to ask who's calling before we give out any information."

I'm not sure if she's telling the truth or not. "And just when is he due back in the office?"

She says, "Mr. Baron will be unavailable for a week. He's out of town." I hear some computer keys clicking. "He's pretty booked when he gets back, but I could give him a note telling him to call you. Would that help?"

I hang up. My letter. Did Mr. Baron even read it before he left? Did he talk to my dad? Probably the answers are no and no. Well, I'm not waiting clear until the end of next week. But what else can I do?

I turn on the computer to keep from going crazy. I find myself Googling the jail. There's a phone number on the Web site to call about visitation. I stare at the digits. Forget that letter. I'm not waiting a week for Baron to get back in town and then who knows how long for him to get back to me. If I show up at the jail, Dad'll be glad I've come. Me and my dad . . . we need each other to begin to make some sense of all this.

At least the media has made it clear which jail has my dad. I dial the phone number. Okay, so I'm nervous, but the person at the jail must talk to lots of inmate's families. Right? But there's not even a human who answers. A computer voice prompts me to the visitation section. She/It tells me that there are visiting hours at that jail from 8:00 to 8:00 on Friday and Saturday. I'll need to bring picture identification, and I'll need to know two pieces of information about the inmate such as birthdate and Social Security number. Then the computer voice reels off a long list of clothing items that can't be worn on a visit. I hang up, feeling stupid for not calling earlier.

We're eating soup again for dinner tonight, but we've made a frozen pizza to go with it. So as I'm putting some extra Parmesan cheese on my pizza, I make a decision. This family, such as we are, needs to stop lying to each other. "Mom," I say. "I'm going to jail to see Dad tomorrow. You don't have to come, but I wanted you to know that I'm doing it. I mean you can come if you want. But I'll understand if you don't."

Mom puts her soup spoon down. "Kev . . . I'm not so sure that's a good . . . "

I interrupt. "Why not?"

Mom says, "I guess . . . I guess I don't like to think of you being in a jail. I mean, I'm sure it's safe and everything, but maybe you should just let the lawyer handle things. Why don't you talk with your dad's lawyer first and see how he feels about your going to see your father?"

I take a deep breath. "I've already talked to Dad's lawyer, and as scary as it feels for me to go to the jail, at least I can leave again. Imagine how Dad feels."

"You talked to his lawyer?" Mom interrupts. "But I don't understand . . ."

I draw a circle of Parmesan cheese on the pizza. I can't look at Mom as I come clean about skipping school to go see Mr. Baron.

"Oh," she says. "I . . . I didn't . . . why didn't you tell me?"

I shrug. "I dunno, Mom. Maybe because no one really tells anyone anything in this family. But I'm trying to change that. That's why I'm telling you this."

If I expect Mom to share a secret in return, it doesn't happen. She tells me how grown-up I seem and how she always wants to know the truth about my life. Then she tries to change my mind about going to the jail. I listen for only a minute before I interrupt her. "I'm going. It's that simple. I'm telling you so I won't be sneaking around your back."

"Okay, then if you must go, I'll go with you. At least you won't be alone."

"Mom, I'll be fine," I say, even though I don't believe it.

My mother shakes her head. "I'm going with you. I'll wait outside when you see your father to make it less awkward if you want." She runs a hand nervously through her hair. "When should we go?"

"Tomorrow," I say.

"But school . . . you've got . . ."

"Mom," I interrupt, "Visiting hours last until 8:00 P.M. I'll go after school."

"No," she corrects, "*we'll* go after school."

It's really an amazing thing that my mother has offered to do for me. I think of how frightened she's been. I don't want her waiting outside a jail—who knows what creepy people may hang out around there, but I don't want her in the visiting room with me and Dad. He needs to be able to tell me what's going on. My head hurts from trying to think how to save everyone.

The phone rings. There have been fewer hate calls lately, so maybe this is a real person. Mom gets up from the dinner table and checks the caller ID. She mouths, "It's work."

They have an extra big data job coming in tomorrow. They want to know if Mom can stay late. I hear her tell them that won't be possible; in fact, she's going to need to leave a little early.

She hangs up. "If you need tomorrow, we'll go tomorrow. I dropped you off for your first day at day camp, your first day at kindergarten, your first day of high school. I guess I'd better keep the tradition up with your first day at jail." She is trying to joke, but the look on her face is much more of a grimace than a grin.

The phone rings again. Mom's work again. They shouldn't have taken on this new job because someone is out sick. Anyway, they will pay her double time and a half if she will cancel her plan to leave early tomorrow night and stay until it's done. Mom says she'll have to get back to them.

"Mom," I ask her, "how bad is our money situation?"

"We're okay." She says, tracing a droplet of soup on the table. I'm not sure that's true, but I can't tackle everything tonight.

Finally, Mom and I compromise. She doesn't want me taking a bus home when it could already be dark out. Truthfully, I'm not so crazy about hanging out at a bus stop by the jail either. So we decide that I'll drop Mom off at work, then go school. After I've visited Dad, I'll go back to her work and wait for her to finish. Neither of us mentions where my car might be.

I pretend to watch TV. I hope I'm pulling off a casual attitude, but the truth is that the whole time,

I'm trying to imagine what it will be like to see my father in a prison uniform.

The next morning, I drop Mom off and go to school in her car. The parking lot is jammed. I don't have my honor student sticker because it's still on the windshield of my missing car, so it's hard to find a spot.

Once inside school, it's like the digital numbers on the classroom clocks are stuck. In Chemistry, I have no partner because Lani hasn't shown up. I am still holding the original beaker I got out when the teacher says it's time to clean up. I realize I never put anything in it. Then school's out, and suddenly, I wish class would have gone on longer.

My legs take me out toward the parking lot. I don't even see Jason, but I guess he's there because suddenly I hear, "Hey. We're going over to the park for a game. You want to come?"

I just shake my head no and keep going. Jason calls, "Hey, we only decided to play at lunch. You weren't around. Don't skip out just because you didn't know about the game."

I don't bother to answer. What's the point? I put my key into the car door lock. I am not going to play basketball or football or baseball. I am going to jail.

I'm counting on my MapQuest directions as I

drive. Not only did I not know where this place was, but until my dad, I didn't even know we had more than one jail. There are four different jails filled with people waiting for trials. I wonder if his is better or worse than the others. How do they decide who gets which jail?

I'm stalled in traffic. There's some kind of traffic jam up ahead, and what should take 15 minutes, takes almost 45. As I get closer, I'm checking the street signs carefully. I don't know my way around here at all. And I've got this weird, awful feeling in my stomach. What if I finally get to see my dad, and I have to pee? Sometimes, when I get really nervous, I keep having to pee. Do they allow you to go to the john if you're visiting a prisoner? Maybe you have to leave and come back. And where do visitors visit? I mean, sometimes on TV, they sit in a room and there's a guard outside, and sometimes, there are all these people sitting in front of a glass with phones, and the visitors have to pick up phones on the other side.

Pretty soon, I recognize the gray concrete building from the picture on the Internet. I drive closer and notice the tall flagpole out in front and the flag waving in the breeze. Yes, sir, step right up to the symbol of freedom and lose it all as you go through the door to jail. Oh, man.

Okay, I'm here. I've got to park the car. But where? I'm not the best parallel parker, so I'll have to find a big spot. Then I notice there're meters at every space. I fish in my pocket for quarters. I feel only one. That won't be enough.

It doesn't matter anyhow because there are no vacant spots. I drive past the front of the ugly building and go north. Maybe there'll be some free parking farther down. I keep driving. I figure I'm about ten blocks from the jail now. I see some guys hanging out on the corner. Not so sure I want to walk past them once it's dark. Not so sure it's a good idea even in the light. I start to circle around to go back closer to the jail. On the other side of the jail, I see a big lot that says Public Parking, and there are even open spaces.

"Okay," I tell myself. "This is good. Everything's going to be okay." I pull in. A guy says, "$5.00," and he raises a bar to the lot.

So I've parked the car. Now, I've just got to make myself open the door and get out. In just a few minutes, I'm going to be standing face-to-face with my father. I tell myself no matter how upsetting it is, I won't let myself look shocked at seeing him in prison. I'm here to give him hope. Truth is, I think I'm here to give us both hope.

I walk up to the front of the jail, past the steel flagpole in front of it, and up the concrete steps. When I get inside, I see signs with arrows. Bail/Bonds. Court Dates. I don't see anything about visitors, but there's a guard near the door. He's chomping on a piece of gum. "Excuse me, sir," I say, "Could you tell me where to go to visit a . . ." It's hard to force the word from my mouth, ". . . a prisoner?"

Guy never even bothers to look at me, just tells me to go outside, around back, and look for the line. "The line?" I question.

He nods. "You'll see it."

I see it okay. I can't believe all of the people waiting. There are whole families here. How many inmates does this jail hold? I walk on and on to find the end of the line. This one is longer than the people waiting for Opus 37 tickets, and everyone wanted those. I stop next to a girl who looks about my age. "Uhm . . . excuse me, is this the line to see all . . . any inmate?"

"Yep," she answers, cracking a piece of gum, "Just keep walking."

I continue to the end of the whole line. I look at my watch. It's already close to 5:00. After all the nervousness, all the buildup—and now I'm just stuck standing in line. Twenty minutes pass. I haven't moved more than a foot. At this point, I'll still be here tomorrow morning. I tap the shoulder of a big guy with a gray ponytail standing in front of me, "Excuse me, you been here before?"

He turns around. "What's it to ya?"

I take a step back. "It's . . . it's nothing. I was just wondering how long this line usually takes."

He spits some tobacco onto the sidewalk and watches as the stain spreads. "Too damn long. I tell my stupid nephew either don't do drugs or don't get caught, but he don't listen." He turns back around.

I stand shifting from one foot to the other. A bunch of kids are chasing each other in a game of tag. It's pretty sad when your playtime is running around waiting to go see your mom or dad in jail. But the kids don't seem to care. "I'm not it," one calls.

"Yes, you are," says a little boy in a T-shirt so big it comes down to his knees.

The guy in front of me spits another wad of tobacco. I wonder if he would save my place so I could go back to the car and get some homework. Might as well get it done while I'm standing out here. Maybe there's a hat in the trunk too. The sun's so bright.

"Uhh . . . excuse me," I say. "Could you, uh, save my place while I go to my car?"

The guy turns around. "You talkin' to me?" I nod. "Save your place," he laughs. "Save your place? Is this third grade?" He laughs again. "Okay, buddy, I'll save your place, if I'm still here when you get back. I ain't waitin' much more." He reaches into his pocket, and sticks more chew into his cheek. I wonder if it's illegal to spit that stuff on the sidewalk, especially right in front of the jail. But he doesn't seem to care. I decide not to chance going to get a hat and homework and having the guy leave while I'm gone. There are a lot more people behind us now, and I'm not going to the back of that line.

About ten minutes later, the gray ponytail shakes his head and says, "This line ain't ever movin'. Stupid kid . . . I can't be doin' this every time he gets himself in trouble." Then just like that, he's gone. I think about his words. He said every time—does that mean he's done this visiting thing a lot and knows we won't get into the jail today? But it's only 6:00. There are two more hours for visiting. Lots of people are still waiting.

"Hey. You got a quarter?" I look down to see a kid staring up at me.

"Huh?"

"I said you got a quarter?" The kid looks to be about eight, with brown hair that hangs almost in his eyes.

"Uh . . . well . . ."

His mother is standing in front of him, and she

turns from hanging on to a baby to tell him to cut it out. He pays no attention to her. "Well, yes or no? You got one?"

I fish in my pocket and pull out the one quarter I have. His hand reaches out and closes over it. "So . . . you want to see a trick?"

"Yeah, okay," I say.

He holds the quarter out in one hand, then closes his hands, puts them behind his back, and puts his closed fists back out in front of me. "Which hand has the money?"

My dad and I used to play this game. I always thought I was so smart. But just as I'm sure Dad did when I was little, I can see a bit of the silver coin through this kid's fingers. "Boy, this is hard," I say to the kid. Then I pick his empty hand.

"Wrong." He shows me the hand with the quarter. "Now watch very good this time."

We play for a few minutes, but after I've gotten it wrong for the fourth time, he says, "Man, are you ever dumb; you always get it wrong." And with disgust, he puts my quarter in his pocket. He tugs on his mom. "I want to go home."

She either ignores him or doesn't hear him as her baby has begun to howl. "Hold your sister," she commands the boy and digs in a diaper bag. She pulls out a pacifier, sticks it in the kid's mouth, and mercifully, the baby stops crying. Then she takes the baby back, and turns to me. "Thanks for trying to entertain Danny."

Danny pipes in, "What . . . I took care of him."

She shifts the baby to her other hip. We've moved up three trees' worth on the side of the path, but there's still quite a ways to the front of the line. "You think we'll make it in?" I ask.

She sighs. "Hard to say. I should've known better. Right after ADC checks is always real crowded."

"What's ADC checks?"

"I know," Danny says. His mother ignores him, explaining to me that those checks mean people have enough money to get gas or bus fare or something to make themselves look better for a visit, so more people show up at the jail. We start to talk a little more. I introduce myself, and she says her name's Candice; her kids are Andrea and Danny. She tells me she's here to see her husband, who is really a good man—he just does some stupid things. She asks me who I'm there to visit. "Uh . . . my *dad*." It's hard to say that, even to someone else in the same situation.

We move up as some people in front of us abandon their places. I ask Candice, "Think they know something we don't?"

Candice sighs, "I should've come earlier. I knew

it. But Danny's teacher threatened to call social services if he was absent again, so I had to wait until school was done today. Then we missed the bus, missed the transfer. But we're here now, and it was such a hassle, I gotta think we'll get in. Just have to have patience."

Danny has none. He is whining. He wants to go home. Candice tells him not to say another word. They're staying. He fishes a ball from his backpack and shows it to me. "Hey, you any better at catch than guessing magic?"

I tell him that actually I think I am. Playing catch with this little kid is better than just standing here, and it's keeping him happy. He moves farther and farther away. He's got a pretty good arm for a little kid, and he seems pretty proud of each catch he makes.

Then the baby starts screaming again. Candice again fishes through her big bag "Oh, no," I hear her say to herself. "Danny," she calls. "We have to go get more formula for Andrea."

But Danny refuses. He sits down on the ground, crosses his legs, and announces that he's not moving. The baby is screaming louder now. Candice turns to me. "Could you just keep playing catch with him until I get back. I'd sure appreciate it."

"Me? Are you kidding?"

The baby is howling. Candice has to shout to be heard over the screams. "I just need to go across the street to buy some formula. You're already playing catch with him, and it's keeping him happy. Besides, are you going anywhere?"

"No," I shout back.

"Okay, then please. I just can't do everything." She looks on the verge of tears. So I say okay, and Candice leaves. Unfortunately, it only takes a few minutes for Danny to tire of playing catch, and I don't know anything about little kids. What do I do if he just takes off? I can't very well go tackle him or something. I keep trying to invent new ways to play catch, which is hard, because after all it's only tossing a ball back and forth.

It seems like forever by the time Candice comes back. But the good news is that the line seems to be moving much faster now. And then movement stops completely. It doesn't make sense, and I say so. Candice explains that visitors get a half hour. Some take the whole thing. Some take only a few minutes, and some people get inside and find out that the person they're visiting has done something wrong and can't have visitors that day. No way of telling what's happening inside, so no way of telling how fast the line will move. A lot of the people who were way behind us have given up and gone home.

Candice says that the longest she ever waited was four hours. I wonder how many times her husband has been here, but I don't ask. We're almost to the bottom of the steps of the building. There are 18 steps. While waiting, I've counted them at least ten times.

Then a man in a blue uniform comes out and stands at the top. "Visiting hours will end in thirty-five minutes." There are some loud boos from the line.

"Thirty-five minutes?" I panic. "But that means we might only have five minutes inside."

Candice shakes her head. "No, that means we're not getting in at all. There're still too many people ahead of us."

"You're wrong," I say. "I'm not just giving up." I can feel my voice crack.

"Well, good luck then," Candice says, starting to gather her stuff. "And thanks for playing catch with Danny. It was a big help. I hope you get in before they close it off." I don't even know this woman, but suddenly, I don't want to walk into that jail by myself.

"Wait. Don't give up now."

"I've got two kids and two buses to catch before I get home. I'm not giving up. I'm just facing reality," Candice says.

"Hey," I reply, "You don't want to take buses from here. It's already getting dark."

Candice shifts the baby on her hip. "Well, my limousine driver is sick, and my Jaguar is in the shop, so I guess the bus is it tonight."

If . . . if you want to wait, I could drive you home," I say impetuously, considering that I have no idea where she lives. "The bus doesn't sound like such a safe idea."

She looks at me with a half-smile, "Oh . . . like it's safer to get a ride with some guy standing at a jail."

"Me," I say. "Are you kidding? I'm fine. Don't I look like a nice guy?"

She stares up at my face. "You look like . . ." She stops and stares harder. "Hmmm . . . like someone I know . . . I think I've seen you before."

"Uhh, I don't think so," I say. I don't want to hurt her feelings, but no way do I normally hang out around jails or people who already have kids who are visiting jails.

Then her face contorts. "Oh, my God. Danny, come here. Right now. You even have the same face. How could I have left my Danny with you?" She grabs his hand, holds her baby to her chest, and rushes from where I am standing.

chapter 13

WHEN I GET TO Mom's work, she sees me walk through the office door, and she immediately clocks out for dinner. She reaches up to stroke my face, "You okay?" she asks. I nod. Her eyes are filled with questions. I don't respond. "Well," she says with fake brightness, "I'm starved. I bet you are too. Let's go eat."

We take the elevator to the company cafeteria, but it's already closed. I guess most people in the building don't work at night. Mom and I head over to Jack in the Box. That stupid clown face smiles at us as we walk through the door. Mom and I stand in line in silence. We wordlessly get our hamburgers, sit down at the table, and I stare at my wrapped food, feeling too unhungry to eat. Mom looks at me, "Did . . . you . . . did you see your dad?"

I shake my head. "No."

"Honey, it's all right. If you decided not to go to the jail, really, it's okay."

I play with the yellow wrapper on my burger. I feel about a hundred years old. "I went. There was a huge long line. Visiting hours were over before I got in."

I can see Mom sigh with relief. She tries to tell me that maybe it was for the best. Maybe I should wait a while before I go back. Maybe I should try to talk to Dad's lawyer first. I listen to all her maybes. I know she's only saying all these things because she cares, but I tell her firmly that I am going back first thing tomorrow morning, and even if I have to wait in line the entire day, I am going to see my father.

We pick at our meal and then return to Mom's office. She's not done until almost 11:30 at night. My body is so tired that it can hardly move itself to get back to the car. On the way home, Mom tries again to change my mind about going back to the jail tomorrow. I know she wants to pretend that none of this happened, but it did. I know she's just trying to protect me, but I need to protect Dad.

She keeps giving me reasons why I shouldn't go back. Finally, Mom says tomorrow won't work because she needs the car. I tell her it's okay. I'll use the bus. She looks at me. I stare back at her. She bites her lip, and quietly asks, "How early do you think you should be in line?"

I really have no idea. Visiting hours don't start until 8:00 A.M., so I arbitrarily pick 7:00. I hope that will be early enough to be near the beginning of the line. "Okay," she says. "Then you'll drop me at work at 6:30 and take the car. You can come back for me later." I try to protest; there's no way she should have to go back to work that early. She won't have been home more than five hours. But Mom only says, "Kevin, you are a remarkable young man and a wonderful son. If I could, I would make it so you never had to go through any of this, but . . ." Her voice trails off and she looks at me with tears in her eyes. "At least take my car."

Yesterday, I didn't even know where the jail was; today, I already feel like a veteran as I park the car and head toward the line. I pass people as I walk, and I wonder if any of them are the newbie I was yesterday, or if they are all veteran visitors. Today, I'm better prepared for the wait. I've got my Gatorade and energy bars.

By the time visiting hours are supposed to start, the line is every bit as long or longer than it was yesterday. But 8:00 comes and goes, and the line hasn't moved an inch.

Finally, the line goes forward. Visiting hours are starting almost an hour late. But I start getting closer to the front, and I can feel my hands sweating. Even if everyone in front of me takes their full thirty minutes, my place in line means I'll still get in to see my dad today. No one is admitted without a government-issued photo ID, so about a hundred times, I pat my back pocket to check that my driver's license is still there.

I recount each of the 18 steps as I get to climb them. The big warning sign about not bringing in food or drink is posted right over the blue barrels beneath it. I throw away my half-eaten energy bar, and then not wanting to take any chances, I toss out my gum too.

The doors open. The guard says he'll be taking the next eight people in line. I am number 7. I am inside the jail.

I show my ID. Like with other visitors they've just admitted, they check to see that my father is there. He is. They check to see that he is eligible to receive visitors. He is. But then as other people are assigned to go to the right into a large visiting room or to the left into a smaller room with phones and plexiglass, I wait.

Finally, a guard comes up to me. "You waiting for #477894?"

"Huh?" I reply.

"Windor, Greg. You waiting for him?"

Suddenly, my voice isn't working so well. "Uh, huh . . . he . . . he's okay, isn't he?"

The guard yawns. "He's okay, okay. He just don't wanna see you."

"What?" my voice rises.

"He don't wanna see you," the guard repeats.

"But did you tell him it was me . . . his son . . . and nobody else?"

He calls another guard over who tells me that the prisoner has been informed of the person who wants to visit him, and the prisoner has refused the visit. That guard adds, "They don't have too many rights around here, but that's one of them. They don't have to see a visitor." He tells me that if I have any further questions, there is an information desk around the front of the building.

I turn and run out of the building, down the steps, and over by the trees where I'd waited for the past two days. Then I barf over and over and over.

I finally pull myself together enough to go home.

That night when I pick Mom up from work, she says, "You okay?"

"Yeah, I'm good."

"It . . . it can't have been easy," she says.

"Yeah, it was tough." I change the subject because

I don't want to tell Mom that Dad wouldn't even see me. "How was work?"

"Kevin, please, don't shut me out. You've just spent two days at a jail."

I don't say anything, but Mom won't let it go. "What did your father say to you? Was he glad you'd come?"

The truth will only reinforce her belief that Dad is a total jerk. I put down the window and let the wind rush by me. I hope the noise will make Mom give up trying to have a conversation. It doesn't. She just keeps asking.

"Okay," I finally say. "You want to know. I'll tell you. I spent two days at that jail, and when I finally got in to visit my father, he refused to see me. Jail guy said that prisoners have that right."

Mom ought to have a field day with that, with what she'll say about Dad deserting people. In fact, I've almost tuned out when Mom says, "Well, maybe Greg truly is capable of loving, totally loving someone after all."

"What?" I explode. "That's love?" I slam my foot on the accelerator, and we barely skid through a light as it turns yellowish-red.

"Kevin, pull over," Mom urges me. "You're too upset to be driving."

"I'm fine," I say, gripping the steering wheel. "It's

the adults in my life who are all screwed up. I have a father who gets himself named the most horrible pervert in the tri-state area, and I've got a mother who thinks he's great for offering me no explanation, for just dismissing me." I cut some guy off as I swerve into his lane, and Mom doesn't say anything more.

When we pull into the driveway, Mom takes a deep breath. She's shaking. "Sorry," I say, unbuckling my seatbelt. "But of all the times to start defending Dad . . ." I can't even finish the sentence.

Mom puts her hand on my arm. "Do you remember that news story about a mother who ran back into her burning house to try to get her baby out? She got badly burned going back in, but she said she had no regrets. It was her child. She had to try."

"And now I'm a baby in a burning building?" I say sarcastically.

Mom looks at me. "No, of course not. But maybe your father has shut you out because he cares as much as that mother did. He doesn't want his son in jails, in courtrooms; his refusing to see you, to make you part of the media frenzy—his trying to keep you out of all that, even when he's sitting in jail—that may be the first truly noble thing your father has ever done."

151

I try to make myself think about what she's said. "So . . . I mean, if that's true . . . if Dad cares about me like that, he couldn't be the monster they're describing, right?"

Mom opens the car door, "Let's go inside. It's been a very long day for both of us."

chapter 14

AND ANOTHER WEEKEND ENDS. Monday, still with-out my car, I'm hoofing it to school when a woman suddenly steps out in front of me on Gold Dust Avenue. "Excuse me," I say. Then I notice. She's holding a microphone, and I see there's a cam-era guy behind her.

"Good morning," she says, "I'm Jenna Eilbert. Could you comment on the upcoming press confer-ence?"

"Huh?" I'm totally in the dark.

She continues, "They've announced a press con-ference at 10:00 A.M. My sources say they'll reveal that they've indicted your father. I believe that means they've found his DNA on the victim. What's your reaction?"

I stand gaping at the camera for a minute, and

then I break into a full run. I don't know if they're going to film my back running away from the reporter and show it on the news. All I know is that I've got to get away. His DNA on the victim? My heart is pounding so hard by the time I get to school that I can't breathe. Is it true? Are they really going to have proof that my dad is the monster? His DNA?

There must be someone at this school who might at least know whether there's really a press conference scheduled for today. I look around. Nothing any different than any other day. No cameras or press hanging out here. But maybe Mr. Leonard would know. He's smart. He pays attention to the news, and he's always been nice to me.

I rush down to room 212. Not much time until school starts. A lot of kids already in his first hour. He looks up. "Ah, Mr. Windor." He's about to crack a joke, but he looks at me again, and suddenly he switches gears. "I need to talk with you about your Thoreau essay, but I'm afraid I've left it in the faculty lounge, so walk with me to get it."

We leave the classroom. "Okay, what's up?" he says. "The look on your face indicates you maybe needed something and didn't want a big audience."

"Did . . . did you listen to the news on your way to school?"

"Yes, I always do."

Why is he making me drag this out of him. "Well," I lick my lips. "Well, did you hear anything about my dad?"

"No, not today,"

"But . . . come on, Mr. Leonard, please be straight with me."

He nods. "One of the newscasters last night said there's speculation that an indictment may be coming soon. But speculation is really just another word for rumor. Even if it happens, an indictment isn't a guilty verdict."

The minute bell rings. Mr. Leonard looks at me. "You going to be okay to go to class?" he asks. "I could send you to the social worker."

"I'm okay. No social worker."

Mr. Leonard nods. "Try to concentrate on school for now. That's all you can do."

He leaves me in the hallway. Should I go home? What if there're more reporters outside. At least they can't get into the school. And Mr. Leonard said that I should concentrate on school. It's the only normal thing left. So I stay.

By fourth hour, there's still no one who's said a word. I've just about convinced myself that the reporter this morning was a tabloid jerk, the kind who reports people snatched to outer space and 50-pound babies being born to 80-year-old women. I tell myself *I'm okay. Dad's okay . . . no indictment, at least not today.*

At lunch, back eating with the guys, I even manage a few jokes. *Just keep trying for normal*, I tell myself. I'm thinking of playing basketball if Jason gets a game after school. Might as well stay busy. In fifth hour, I'm fiddling around with my pen when the little top push-down piece pops off and rolls somewhere on the floor. My dad gave me that pen. It cost over $100! He told me that I had great ideas, and I should have a great pen to write them down. So I wait until class is out, and I look under desks until I finally see a small piece of silver glinting two rows over. Nice trajectory. I pick it up; the warning bell rings. Cripe. I've got one minute to make it to class. I shove the pen piece into my backpack to fix later. Anyone who's tardy to Leonard's class has to sing, and I don't want to be standing in front of his class singing. My motto these days is no extra attention to myself.

I'm rushing, but I can't miss the couple in the stairwell; they're practically inhaling each other. As I pass, I think that guy looks awful familiar, and I realize . . . it's Jason. Way to go, buddy! The guy who's so shy around girls suddenly seems to be communicating real well. And then I realize whose face he's kissing.

I storm up the stairs and into Leonard's class. So what, I tell myself. So what. Ironically, I make it before the bell rings, but Jason arrives late for class. "Pass, Jason?" Mr. Leonard says.

Jason just has this dumb grin on his face as he shakes his head no. "Well, you're three minutes late. What's the song for three minutes?"

The class looks to Stacey Hemel, who always keeps track of the trivia. 'Itsy Bitsy Spider,' she says.

"No problem," Jason replies, and he sings away. He looks so happy it's disgusting. As Jason finishes his song, Leonard sighs. "You look like a man in love, which is all good and fine, but it better not mean any more tardies to my class."

I try to see what Leonard's writing on the board about Thoreau, but all I see is Jason, my best friend, hooking up with Emily. Block it out, I tell myself. I try to listen to Leonard talk about *Walden*, but the tabloid reporter's voice is too loud. Over and over, I hear it. *DNA. Indictment. My father. My best friend. My supposed-to-be girlfriend.*

I feel my chair shoved, and Jason is standing next to me. "Time for group work." He punches me lightly on the arm. "Hey, come out of la-la land!"

I don't even know I'm doing it. My eyes and my ears are filled with everything that's wrong and suddenly fists find Jason's face. I feel hands grabbing at me. I resist. Finally, the hands grip me so I can't move. Three guys are hanging onto me. Jason is sitting on the floor. He's bleeding above his right eye and out of his mouth. Someone hands him a tissue. He spits blood. The rest of the class is frozen, watching. Leonard barks, "Show's over. Get back in your groups and get going on the Thoreau assignment."

He takes me and Jason outside. "I'm okay," Jason says. "Just let it go." Only it's hard to understand him because his lip is so swollen.

Mr. Leonard looks at me. "I know your life has been awful these last few weeks, but you attacked Jason with no provocation. You could be looking at expulsion. It's assault. I just . . ." He stops and shakes his head. "I'm sorry, but I have to report this."

Jason looks at Leonard. He has to tilt his head to see the teacher through the eye I didn't hit. He says, "Look, if you have to report it, tell them I started it."

Mr. Leonard says he can't do that—it would be a lie—but he'll try to figure out something. He tells me I'm really lucky to have a friend like Jason. Then he takes his cell phone from his pocket. "I need an escort for two boys from room 212. I'll be down to fill out the paperwork after class."

Jason wipes some blood from his lip with the back

of his hand. He looks awful, but I think I feel even worse. How could I have done this? "Jason, I . . . I am so sorry . . ." He doesn't answer.

A guy from maintenance comes, and Leonard goes back into his classroom. The maintenance guy says, "I'm gonna walk between you two, and I don't want you guys talkin' any trash. I don't even want neither one of you lookin' at each other. Got that?"

Our school doesn't have enough problems for a resource officer, so escorting us is probably a break for the maintenance guy from having to mop the cafeteria floor.

Jason is dropped off at the nurse while I find myself sitting on the office bench. I am there for what seems like forever. The bell for the end of the hour rings, for the start of the next hour, and then finally for the end of school, but I'm still sitting there. I haven't seen Jason again, which I hope is because they're just keeping us apart, and not because he is really hurt.

Finally, I see Mr. Leonard stride into the office. Maybe he can tell me about Jason. "Mr. Leonard . . ." But that's all I get out before I am interrupted. "Just sit there and not one word," he commands, continuing to Dean Kenter's office.

I don't know exactly what it is that Mr. Leonard says, but when I am called into the dean's office, I'm told that I will take an anger management class that starts next week after school; until then, I'm suspended for the rest of this week. I'm not expelled unless I ever get into a fight again at Chapparal High. I have to sign a paper that says I agree to everything. I sign and say, "Please don't suspend Jason. He didn't do anything. He didn't even throw a punch to protect himself."

The dean doesn't answer about Jason. She only says that I am very lucky. I could have been arrested for assault. I could have been expelled for an unprovoked fight, and I'd better get it together because this is my last chance not to make a mess of my life.

"Okay. Thanks," is what I say. What I think is, *Not make a mess of my life? Are you kidding me? Have you tried living a life where everyone thinks your dad is a monster, and you may be too?*

Mom is totally freaked that I'm suspended again. When they call her to school to check me out, she practically has her own breakdown. I'm embarrassed. And I feel bad. The whole punch-out with George was one thing. I had no choice—fight or get killed. But Jason?

On the way home, Mom keeps sniffling and wiping her eyes at every stop light. And I wonder what kind of jerk I am. All I've accomplished is to make my mom cry and beat up a guy who wouldn't even fight back. More proud moments in the life of Kevin Windor.

I tell Mom I'm sorry. She sighs. She tells me she knows—she knows I'm a great kid, but there are still tears running down her cheeks. When I get home, I head into my room, pull out my cell, and stare at it. I open and close the phone about a hundred times before I finally make myself hit number 1 on speed dial. I have no idea what to say, so I hope I can just leave a message. But I hear Jason's "Lo?"

I take a deep breath. "Jason, I'm so sorry. I hope you're okay. I swear, man, I didn't mean to hurt you. I didn't even know I was going to hit you." There's silence. I take the phone away from my ear to see if the call ended, but the timer is still going. "It was just that there was some stuff on the way to school this morning and . . . uh . . . then there was . . . the stairwell thing. Look, I called to say thanks for trying to keep me from getting expelled by saying you started the fight. I want you to know I told the dean it was all me."

Still nothing. I continue. "So . . . uh . . . no matter how much you're with Emily, the fighting stuff . . . it won't happen again."

Finally, Jason speaks. "Don't worry about it."

"You okay?" I ask.

"Yeah, nothing's broken."

"Great. That's really great." I'm relieved that at least I didn't do anything terrible to him. "And you're not suspended, right?"

"Right."

"Well, that's good. You don't deserve to be."

"Okay."

"Okay . . . so then we're okay, right?" I ask.

There's a pause before he says, "Yeah, sure, we're okay."

"Good. How about next b-ball game, you give me a sharp upper cut when you block my shot."

But Jason says he thinks maybe we should take a break from hanging out. It'd probably be better if he just sees me around.

"Sure, whatever's good for you." I close the phone. I should never have hit him. No way. No excuses. And I'm sorry. I really am. But the whole Emily thing—shouldn't he say he's sorry about that?

So . . . here I am. Suspended. It's me and *The Price Is Right*. Again. And again, I've messed up everything. This week, Mom had really been looking forward to going to Albuquerque for a training meeting for the entire week. It was her first chance to travel, and she was so excited. She was still going—her job required it. But instead of being excited, she was in tears when she left, worried about me. Another of my proud moments.

I am ashamed of myself over practically knocking out my best friend, and I'm ashamed of myself for destroying my mom's working vacation, but I'm even more ashamed of what I'm planning to do next.

I try to rationalize. I mean, I've already searched through Dad's stuff in his house, so I guess I'm already an awful person. I enter Mom's room. Has she thrown away everything that was about her and Dad, or is there still something that will help me understand the difference between the monster they talk about in the media and the father I knew? Is there something hidden in here that will explain the reason my dad refused to see me? Whether this helps my one-man effort to free my innocent father or reveals the worst, I've got to know. I take a deep breath and open the first of Mom's dresser drawers. Just clothes. And the same is true of the other drawers in the small dresser.

I move from the dresser, open Mom's closet, and catch a whiff of her cologne. I almost expect to turn around and see her, which only adds to my guilt. Her closet isn't all that big, so it doesn't take me long to look through it, and I'm just about to shut the door when, on the floor, I see one box smaller than the other shoe boxes. I'm not sure why, but I reach down and push off the lid. The box is filled with papers and photos. Carefully, I pick up and carry the small blue box from Mom's room to my own. It's stupid because there's no one else in the house except me; in fact, Mom isn't even in the same state. Still, I shut the door to my bedroom before I dump the box onto my bed. The first paper in it is a recipe. Great. I've invaded Mom's privacy for recipes. But then I pick up another piece of paper—a marriage license from the state of Georgia. So there is some remnant of my father in all this. I begin turning over each piece of paper. Notes my father wrote to my mother while they were in high school! Wow. He sounded so in love with her. How did the kid who wrote these notes just stop loving that girl?

A photo of my mom and dad from when they eloped. The boy whose arm is around the girl looks just like me. And Mom, she was pretty—did she ever really look that young?

I put the photo down and pick up a copy of a traffic ticket that Dad had gotten on their way back from Georgia. Then another photo of Mom and Dad. In this one, my smiling father has his hand on Mom's bulging stomach. On the back, small blue script indicates, "Our first apartment, and me seven months pregnant!" I look at the photo again. Mom sitting on an old sagging sofa with cinderblocks for end tables sporting two mismatched lamps, one with no shade.

I think of Dad's condo now: big butter-soft leather sofas, special ergonomic chairs for his computers, and amazing electronics. Hard to believe he'd ever lived in that dump in the photo. But he's smiling in the picture.

There's a copy of the divorce decree and a piece of blue satin. I don't know what the blue satin is for. And there's a pair of baby shoes that must have been mine. That's it. The total of my parents' life together. There's something so very sad about the whole thing.

As I put the stuff back into the box, I stare at the wedding picture again. Those two smiling kids—my parents. They thought life was going to be great. But look how things have turned out.

As I'm putting the papers back, I see an envelope I missed. It is stamped *return to sender* and is still un-opened. I stare at the name and address. It can't be. Even if it is, he probably doesn't live there anymore. Maybe he isn't even still alive. But then again . . . I stare at the envelope harder. That name . . . it has to be—he is Dad's own flesh and blood. The envelope sits in my hand. Why did my mother write to my father's father? Why didn't he open it? And why has she kept it?

I have to open the envelope carefully enough to

seal it again. I work at one corner. It won't give. I try the other side. The envelope starts to tear. No way I can get it open and reseal it. To get to the letter, I'll have to destroy the envelope. I stare at it again.

What do I do? I haven't learned anything from the rest of this stuff, so the letter's probably not going to help either. Maybe Mom just told my grandfather off. Good for her if she did. The men in our family have done a job on her. I guess that's why in the end, I don't open the envelope. It's not worth her knowing that her son betrayed her too. But as I put the envelope away, I stare at the front. Donald Windor. He has a name now and a street address. Maybe he still lives there. And maybe he's sorry now for making everything so hard for Dad. Maybe he hasn't come forward because he's afraid Dad wouldn't want him now. But maybe, if he knew we needed help . . .

All night I toss and turn thinking. About 5:00 in the morning, I get up and Google my grandfather's name. Nothing shows up. Then I go to whitepages.com and try the name and address on the envelope. I don't really expect to see a match. But it's there—my grandparents in the same house my dad grew up in!

By 7:00, I've taken the keys to Mom's car. I drive over to Dad's, and I let myself in. This time, Mr. Seibert isn't outside. Must be too early for him. This time, I haven't come looking for old memories or new evidence. I've come because I need cash. If I'm going to Boise, I have to do it before my mom returns from Albuquerque and before my suspension from school ends. And all that can't happen without gas money, which I am fresh out of. Mom never leaves any spare cash in the house; I'm not sure she has any to leave, but Dad often has some extra twenties lying around.

For just a minute, I almost expect Dad to be in his office working on some computer game or flopped on the sofa watching his new TV. Everything looks so normal.

From all the times we've ordered pizza, I know the most likely places to look for cash. I find a fifty in the kitchen junk drawer. There are four twenties rolled together and stuck into the pens cup on Dad's desk and a twenty lying out on the desk. That's $150—should be enough. I'm anxious to get going.

I MapQuest driving instructions. Mom's car is kind of a junker with 80,000 miles on it and only the factory-installed radio. No CD player, no Satellite. But at least Mom's car is here. Who knows if I'll ever see my or Dad's car again.

I've got to cover 960 miles to get from Phoenix to Boise. I figure that's two days of driving there and two back, which means I can just about make it back to Phoenix in time to pick up my mom from Sky Harbor Airport. At first, I'm really nervous about even the thought of meeting my grandparents. What do you say to relatives you didn't know existed? And what do you say when your common bond is a man that the world is calling a monster?

After nine hours of nonstop driving, except for one fast food and pee break, my butt is numb, and I'm barely thinking at all. I pull into a place called Mesquite, Nevada. Neon lights beckon from a casino. I make a quick decision. If I can sneak into one, I'll gamble ten bucks. If I win, I'll get a room. If I don't, I'll drive until I can't stand it anymore. Then I'll pull into one of those highway rest stops and sleep in the car.

I lock the car. It feels so good to walk around. Neon lights flash brightly. I walk into a casino and see a sign on the wall that no one under 21 is allowed. But no one pays any attention to me. I go up to the cashier and get two tens for a twenty. I don't want to gamble too much.

I've never tried a slot machine before. I put a ten into the machine and push the button. Pretty soon, I'm up to $13. A profit but not enough. I need to bet more to win more. Next thing I know, the whole ten is gone along with the $3 profit. I tell myself to quit, but I'm really tired and Mom's old car is not going to be good for sleeping. So I fish in my pocket for the other ten. And then I lose and lose again. I'm so disgusted I bet it all.

And then bells and sirens ring. It's not the big jackpot, but I've won $500, and given my current financial situation, that's huge. A guy materializes at the machine next to me. "You underage . . . you lose it all. I claim it—costs you 50% of the win, but at least you get half."

"But . . ." I start to say, and the guy cuts me off, says now, or it'll be too late. A cashier comes over, and he gives her my winning slip. She gives him the $500, and I'm sure I'm going to get stiffed. Then the guy walks outside the casino, and I follow hoping he hasn't just taken off with my money. But if he has, what can I do? Say he's stealing the money I broke the law to win? But he's waiting for me; he peels off $250, and says, "Lucky for you I came along when I did."

So I'm rich enough to stay in a hotel tonight, and my room is pretty good. I mean it's not like the suites my dad has described, but it's nice enough. I should be able to sleep. Only it doesn't work that way. I stare at the ceiling all night, trying one introduction after another to the strangers who are my grandparents, wondering if they've ever thought about me all this time. I start out the next morning feeling like crap. For all the sleep I've gotten, I could have stayed in Mom's car and saved my money.

I continue the drive into Boise. Almost there, I pull off into a fast food joint. I figure I should eat something. I buy a breakfast burrito, look at it, feel the bile coming up from my stomach, and toss the meal uneaten into the trash. Sipping some water, I realize I've been so intent getting to Boise that I haven't thought enough about the man I'm about to meet. My grandfather destroyed my parents' marriage and hated my mom for no good reason. How can I really expect to get any help from him?

But who knows what really happened way back then? Who knows if the story Linda told me is true at all? In fact, my grandparents may be glad to see me. They may have wanted to meet me for a long time.

I try practicing what I should say when one of them answers the door. I wonder if it will be my grandfather or my grandmother. I turn from the Parkway onto State and double-check the directions, though I've read them so many times that I've memorized them. Just two more right turns, and I should be on the street where my dad grew up, where he walked away from his house, his parents, and his life as he knew it.

In some ways, I wish I could do the same. I could keep going from here, head to California, where they have so many crazy things going on that my dad would probably not even make the news. I could start over there. I'd disappear in Mom's car. I'd walk out on her just like my dad. But I can't do that.

I pull up in front of the house two doors down from the one that is supposed to contain my grandparents. Maybe I should have put on a shirt and tie to meet them. Do I call them Mr. and Mrs. Windor or Grandma and Grandpa? Maybe I shouldn't introduce myself at all at first.

I force my legs out of the car and propel my feet in a forward direction toward the address on a letter more than a decade old. I open the gate of the white picket fence and walk past a large maple tree up to a neatly painted blue front door. Matching blue shutters frame each window. The house is not large, but it looks like it belongs on Disneyland Main Street. How could such an old-fashioned, all-American house have produced such sadness?

My hand reaches out; my finger presses the bell. I gulp air. Why did I ever decide to do this? But I can't leave. My feet are now so riveted to the welcome mat that I can't move. Seconds or maybe hours pass before I realize that no one has answered the doorbell's chime. No one is coming. No one is home. Okay. I've tried. I'm going to get back in the car and return to Phoenix.

I turn and start back toward the car. I'm about halfway to the street when I hear a voice call, "Yes, did you just ring our bell?" I am tempted to break into a full run to the car, but some invisible force holds me. I turn around and begin my way back to the front door. "Yes . . . yes, Ma'am, I did. You see . . ."

But I don't get any further than that. She screams, "Donald! Oh, Donald, come!" and then she faints. I sprint through the doorway and bend down to check to make sure she's okay. I'm still bending over my grandmother when I hear a gruff voice demand, "I've got a gun right on you, and if I shoot, I won't miss, so you stand up, and you move away from my wife."

"But I didn't, I mean you don't . . ." I lift my head, put my hands in the air, and begin to stand.

Before I can begin to explain, my grandfather looks at me full on. "Oh, dear Lord," he says. He puts the gun down. "Greg?" The word comes out in a gasp.

chapter 15

THE NEXT FEW MINUTES are so chaotic, I'm not quite sure in what order things happen myself. All I know is that afterward I am sitting at a rough-hewn oak kitchen table with a glass of lemonade placed on a sunny yellow placemat. My grandfather has realized that, of course, I cannot be his son as he was many years ago. And then I think he's embarrassed, and then he's angry.

But then, it comes to them that I must be who I am. That should make things less awkward, but it seems to evoke total silence. It's like there's so much to talk about . . . where to begin?

Finally, my grandfather speaks. "How old are you?" It seems a strange opening. I mean he knew when my mom was pregnant. But I answer that I just turned 17.

"What's your name?" my grandmother asks.

I tell her that it's Kevin.

She gasps. "Kevin," she looks at me. "Kevin was your Dad's uncle's name. He was in the army—killed in the war." Teary-eyed, she turns to my grandfather. "Donald, they named him after my brother."

My grandfather doesn't respond to that. Instead, he asks me, "You a good student?"

"Yes, sir." That sounds like bragging. "I mean, I'm not the best in the world, but I'm pretty good."

He nods, "You take AP classes?"

"Yes, sir."

"You got a girlfriend?"

I think of Emily and swallow a lump. Why do I still care about that girl? "No, sir," I say forcefully. "No girlfriend."

"Good!" he states emphatically.

I've been studying my grandfather. He doesn't look much like my dad or me. It isn't just the white hair either. He barks out questions, and I feel like I have to answer. I hope he's almost done, so I can get the conversation to my dad and how we can help him.

But my grandfather's questions continue. "You know where you want to go to college?"

"I'm not exactly sure yet."

"Where are you thinking?" he asks.

"Well, maybe Stanford or Yale." I can feel my grandfather's piercing blue eyes. "Uhm, I mean I may not get in those schools, but Dad says the sky's the limit, dream big. So, right now . . . I'm dreaming." That wasn't the way I planned to bring up Dad.

My grandmother puts her hand to her mouth. "That's just what . . . what your grandfather used to say to your father."

Her husband bangs his hand on the table. "Before he threw it all away. Before he ruined his life. Running off with that girl. Where is he now? Nowhere. That's where his stupid mistakes led."

I realize they didn't ask me to come here, and I am sitting at their table, but that girl is my mother, and she is not the problem. I feel a dark flush creeping up my face. "Mom and Dad got divorced a long time ago. And my mother is a terrific person. She didn't do anything wrong." Now that I'm started, I can't seem to stop. "I came here because Dad really is in trouble. You may not know it, but he's been a great dad. He needs help now, but I'm just a kid. You're his parents. You're the only other flesh and blood he's got. Where have you been? Why haven't you tried to talk to his lawyer, to help him?"

My grandfather looks me in the eyes. "Your father died at age 17. The young man we knew as our son perished when he walked out of this house, threw away the hopes and dreams of a whole community, and for what . . . sex."

I break in. "They were in love."

My grandfather pushes his chair from the table and begins pacing. "Don't give me that. This is not some stupid teenage movie. What do you know about the man you call your father? Has he ever even talked about himself in high school?" I don't say anything, and my grandfather continues. "I didn't think so. Well, let me tell you. Your father was the brightest young man Boise High had ever seen. MIT, Cal Tech, the nation's top schools were recruiting him by his junior year. It wasn't just the perfect math score on the SAT when he was just a sophomore. He took the ACT as a junior. Perfect score on that one too. That boy had it all. Handsome, well-rounded, well-liked, and a real-life genius. School counselors told us some day, we'd be watching him get the Nobel Prize or something equally grand. We weren't rich, but we were going to do whatever it took to give that boy all the education he ever wanted. 'Dream big,' we told him. 'Dream big.' Everybody in our little community was excited. He was going to be the star for everyone to be proud to have known him when he was just a boy. Mayor told me one day at church, he wouldn't be surprised if they had to rename city hall some day."

I'm sort of fascinated in spite of everything. I mean I knew Dad was smart, and Mom's friend had said he was the best student at Boise High, but this renaming city hall . . . no matter how much people say we're alike, I know that no mayor is ever going to talk about one day renaming city hall after me. I mean, I'm not dumb, but no one ever thought I was some kind of genius. My grandfather sits down again, his tirade seemingly exhausting him. "So he gave it all up for that piece of trash."

"She's not . . ."

He interrupts. "Did you know that she lived with her grandmother because her own mother wouldn't stick around, was too busy partying somewhere? Did you know that her own grandmother was so ashamed of their running off like that, that she came to church and apologized to me and my wife?"

My grandfather is turning bright red. My grandmother puts a hand on his arm, but he shakes it off. "Well, big surprise for that little gold digger. Thought she latched onto a potential Midas in getting her hooks into my son, but thanks to her, he was broke with no future."

I push my chair back and stand up. I want the height over my seated grandfather. I feel like screaming at him, but I keep my voice even. "And here's what you don't know about *that girl*. My mom works long hours for little pay because instead of going to college herself, she stayed home to take care of me while Dad finished school. And you also don't know that even though my mom loved him so much, one day he just decided he didn't want to be married and walked out on her. And you don't know that my dad lives really well now in a house much nicer than yours, but my mom—she struggles all the time. And you don't know that I've always treated my dad like the hero, and my mom like a pest or a pain, but . . . but somehow, my mom . . ." I stop and take a breath. I'm NOT going to cry in front of these people. "Somehow, in spite of everything, my mom loves me anyway."

My grandmother stands next to me and pats my arm. "It's a good quality to love your mother. You're a kind boy to defend her. I think we all need to stop talking about the past. It's over. We didn't mean for you to get so upset." She encourages me to sit down again. "We're very glad you've come to visit. Your grandfather and I have wondered about you so many times." She turns to my grandfather. "It's almost a miracle, isn't it, Donald? They look so much alike. Oh, my . . . it's as if Greg is sitting right here with us again."

My grandmother begs me to stay a bit longer. Part of me wants to walk out on these people . . . treat them the way they treat my mom. But they're the only other relatives I've got. If they like me enough, maybe they'll help me clear my father. I can't do it alone. Maybe because they're old, they've let themselves forget how much they once loved Dad. Maybe I can't hit them over the head with it all at once.

We visit for a long time, but we say so little. When I tell them I need to get going, my grandfather insists that I stay for an early dinner, so I do. And then at dinner, they want me to stay the night. But I'm not going to. I feel like it would be betraying my mom to stay the night with people who said and did such awful things to her. Like it's not betraying her that I've taken her car and come here without telling her. Okay, so I don't make much sense. I just don't want to stay the night.

However, my grandmother pleads with me that she's really worried about me driving such a long distance in the dark. I say I'll be fine, but my grandfather sweeps away my assurances and announces that I will be staying. He just orders it, and honestly, I don't have enough energy left to fight him. I tell myself there's no point to making a scene. I can leave first thing in the morning; they'll be happy and my mom won't be any the wiser.

So I spend the night in my father's old room. It feels so strange. There's a bulletin board still filled with his high school awards, and his desk drawers are still filled with college catalogs and graded homework from 30 years ago.

Grandma comes into my room, allegedly to see if there's anything I want. She looks around. "Somehow, it just seems so right to see you in here," she says. She fluffs the pillow on the bed and explains that at first they were so sure Dad would come back home that they left everything alone, and then when he didn't, they were too upset to remove all his things. So I guess they pretty much just shut the door and erased the room from their lives as well as the boy who'd lived there.

Grandma says it means the world that I've come. She asks if I would mind if she gave me a hug, and I say it would be okay. After she's gone, I sit on the bed trying to imagine myself as Dad. In his closet, there are still a bunch of sweatshirts from colleges he'd been considering. Yale and Stanford are on the top of the pile. I lie down, but I don't sleep much—I feel like I've stepped back into someone else's life. Sort of a time travel without the fun of it.

The next morning, Grandma–that word still sounds weird to say–makes me breakfast, and my grandfather invites me to stay on for more than just another evening. I almost feel as if he wants me to come and live out my dad's senior year and create the college experience that my dad should have had.

Before my grandfather tries to take control again, I tell him that I have to leave *today*, and then I take a deep breath and plunge forward, "Will you both come back to Phoenix with me and meet with Dad's attorney? I think it might really help Dad. This attorney, he doesn't pay attention to me, maybe because he thinks I'm just a kid. But if we all went in, if we all demanded better information . . ."

Grandma's eyes open wide, and she looks to my grandfather.

"Please," I say. "Please. Don't you think your son deserves justice?"

Suddenly, Grandpa, who has been so forceful in knowing just what I should do, gets vague. And even my kindly grandmother won't commit to helping my father. How can parents just totally turn away from their child, I wonder. But then I think again. Isn't that what my father has done to me?

The best I can get from the senior Windors is a "We'll think about it." There are hugs from Grandma, pleading for me not to be a stranger, and a firm handshake from my grandfather, telling me he's proud that I'm staying focused on college. They say they just have to get a few things in order, and they'll call me. I give them my cell phone number. It might be a little weird for Mom to have to answer their call at home.

Then I'm on the road. The miles fall away. I'm thinking about how it's always been just me, Dad, and Mom. Now, I have grandparents. I know it's been a long time since they've let themselves think about Dad, but now that I've talked to them, I hope they'll see how much he . . . how much I need them to help.

One thing about my grandfather, he wouldn't be easily put off by that lawyer or the police or anyone. His stubborn gruffness would be just what we need. And then Dad, after he gets out, he'd find out how much Grandpa helped him, and they could . . . suddenly, a horn blares from behind me, and a green F-150 pickup truck swerves around on two wheels. In front of me now, the guy holds up his middle finger in his rearview window. What a jerk.

The miles stretch on, as does the boring scenery. I try to imagine what it was like to grow up in my dad's house. Was my grandfather always so . . . so sure about everything? Did it always have to be his way? I think of the easygoing relationship Dad and I have always had. Was it ever that way for Dad with his own father?

More miles behind me, but I'm barely even aware of the number I've covered until I'm back in Mesquite. I realize that I haven't stopped to pee in far too long, and I need more gas. I'm not really hungry, but eating seems like a break from driving, so I find a gas station, a bathroom, and a restaurant. Los Lupes is probably not the fanciest restaurant in Mesquite, but the burritos look amazing. I'm not that hungry, but my burrito tastes so good that I eat the whole thing.

I'm feeling a little better by the time I get back in the car; I think maybe I can drive straight through to Phoenix. I'd just as soon sleep in my own bed. It's just too bad that Mom's car radio signal keeps fading in and out, but I leave it on. Sometimes the stations come in, but mostly they're static.

I cross the border into Arizona, and the radio springs to life with a country western song about a man who lost his dog and his girl. I think that's nothing. I seem to have lost a father and a life.

My hands feel welded to the wheel, but I push on. Finally, I pull over to the side of the road, get out for a couple of big stretches, and then I'm back in the car until my blurry eyes see my own house. I go into my room, strip off my sweaty clothes, fall into my bed, and completely crash.

The next time I look at the blue numerals of the clock next to my bed, I realize that I've slept for 12 hours. I jump into the shower. I have to get to the airport. My butt is not happy to be back in the car. I look at the gas gauge. Almost empty, better not chance it. I stop for gas and race toward the airport. Amazingly, I make it before my mom's plane lands. And when she comes out of baggage, I'm waiting at the curb. She hugs me. "I missed you. You doing okay?"

"I'm fine," I say.

"Were you terribly bored?" she asks.

"Not so much," I reply. "Tell me about Albuquerque."

chapter 16

I'S YET ANOTHER MONDAY morning. My trip to Idaho is still a secret from my mom. My suspension has ended, and I have to go back to school. Before I leave, my mom begs me not to get in any more trouble. The dean has made it clear to both of us that this is my very last chance.

I promise. As I walk back into school, I wonder what the rumor mill has been churning out about me during my last suspension. Whatever it is, I'll just have to deal with it. I'm not fighting again!

It's a lonely day. I don't speak to anyone; I don't look at anyone. I slide into my seat in every class and keep my head down. When I'm buying my piece of pizza, I glance over for a minute to Jason's table, and then I take my pizza outside to eat by myself.

Leonard calls on me twice in English. I know the

answers to both questions. He tells the class the answers are insightful, thoughtful. Maybe. Or maybe he's just trying to make me feel a little better. Who knows?

Finally, it's the end of the last hour. It hasn't been a great day, but at least people have just pretty much ignored me. That's better than what I thought might happen.

On my way out of school, I see Jason talking to a group about a pick-up basketball game. He sees me, but he doesn't say anything. *Who cares?* I tell myself. I have too much makeup work to do anyway.

As I walk home, I check my cell phone again. My grandparents haven't called. Dad doesn't want to see me. His lawyer doesn't want to talk to me, and apparently, his own parents don't want to help. Even the media has gone on to cover other breaking news stories. Maybe there's a message in all that. Maybe it's time for me to stop carrying Dad around on my back every single day. I wonder, could I really let go of it for a while? It doesn't mean that I think my father is guilty. It doesn't mean that I won't help him. It just means a break—freedom for a little while.

When I get home, I make myself a big snack, and my cell phone rings. As I flip it open, I see it's an in-state area code, and I don't recognize the number. I answer. A woman's voice, "Is this Kevin Windor?"

I've become smart enough not to answer that. "Who's asking?"

"I'm calling on behalf of Mr. Baron, of the law firm . . ." and then she starts with the whole laundry list of names.

"Yeah, this is me." I say.

"Please hold for Mr. Baron." Then his voice comes on the line. "Good afternoon, Kevin. I've received permission from your father to share the following information with you. At 6:00 P.M. this evening, the District Attorney's office is calling a press conference. We have every reason to believe that they will announce that your father's DNA was found at the scene and on the victim, and we believe they will announce that the grand jury has come back with multiple indictments against him."

I can't breathe. I gulp. "Does . . . that mean my dad is . . . he's . . . he's the DB25?"

"Not at all," the lawyer says. "I will announce that your father is pleading not guilty to all charges. We will be mounting a vigorous defense on his behalf."

How can the lawyer be so matter-of-fact? He could be announcing the morning weather. "Oh." I can't think of what else to say. I can't think at all. "Does . . . does Dad want to see me now?"

The lawyer clears his throat. "Not at this time."

"Not at this time?" I explode. "So when does he want to see me? When is he going to explain all this?"

The lawyer continues, "As much as he wishes he could stop it, Mr. Windor now believes that he cannot keep the media from approaching you. My suggestion to you would be to talk as little as possible, and if cornered with a question you cannot escape, say only that you love your father, you are sure he's innocent, and you have no comment about anything else."

"But . . . but if he's innocent, then why is Dad's DNA . . .?" I can't finish the statement. I've listened to the news. I know the way the DB25 hacked up some of those women and then left them to die a slow, painful death. How did my father's DNA get on one of the DB25 Monster's victims?

Mr. Baron's smooth voice never even sounds distressed as he assures me that there could be many reasons why Dad's DNA is on the scene. He reminds me that I must have learned in school that a person is innocent until proven guilty, and just because a person is charged with a crime does *not* mean he committed it.

But this isn't some hypothetical person in some Government class. It's my dad, and it doesn't make any sense. "I want to see my father! He's got to at least see me," I demand.

Mr. Baron isn't moved. "I'm afraid that will not be possible for now."

"I'll be in court. I'll be in court every day. My father cannot avoid me forever. Tell him that. Tell him. I deserve to understand what's happening. I want my father to talk to me." I'm gripping my cell phone so hard.

Mr. Baron's calm voice: "Understood. We'll work on that, but you needn't feel such a sense of urgency. Even if there is a trial, it won't happen for at least a year. For now, the best thing you can do is just try to avoid the press for a few days until news of the indictment has faded away."

"Please. Tell him I want to see him now. Tell him I tried to go to the jail to see him. If . . . if he didn't do these awful things, please tell him I just need to hear it from him."

Mr. Baron sighs. "Kevin, you must understand that your father's silence does not indicate his guilt. His not wanting to see you may only be his way of sparing you from involvement in all this, and . . ."

I don't let him finish. "Then tell him it isn't helping. Tell him I'll survive the tabloids, and I'll be fine. I just need to hear from Dad that he isn't some kind of monster. And I need to know from him why he wrote that letter saying he was pleading guilty."

Mr. Baron's voice takes on a firm edge. "Your father is pleading not guilty. If you are searching for an answer, you have it. Not guilty. The rest is best left to letting us prepare the best defense that we can. And we have our reasons for what we do."

"That's not enough. Do you have any idea what my life has become?"

"At the risk of being harsh, it's not *your* life that is our main concern, is it?" says Mr. Baron.

The call ends. I stare at the phone as if I can't believe the words that have just come from it. The DNA—Dad's DNA—that was supposed to prove him *not guilty* . . . instead, it was *his* DNA found on that woman . . . and on how many other DB25 victims? "Oh, Dad," I scream.

Numbly, my fingers dial my mom's work number. "Come home," I order. I am amazed at how steady my voice is. Mom starts to ask what's the matter. She sure hopes I'm not in more trouble, am I? I cut her off. "Come home, now," I say and hang up the phone. I can't get any more words out.

As soon as I get the receiver down, the phone rings again. I let the machine answer. "Kevin, pick up. Kevin, what's wrong?" asks Mom.

But no way—I can't make myself deliver the news about Dad's DNA over the phone. "Kevin?" Mom's voice speaks into the machine again. When I still don't reply, I hear, "Kevin, I'm coming home right now. I'll be there real soon. Don't do anything foolish."

Mom does get home really fast, or I'm in such a suspended state that I don't know how long it has taken. She rushes in and throws her arms around me. "Oh, thank God!" she says, "I was afraid you'd . . ."

"It's Dad, his DNA," I force out. "They found it on . . ."

Mom crumples onto the sofa. "No," she whispers.

And like when you hear the crash of a bad car wreck, but you can't look away, we turn on the TV at 6:00 P.M. The news conference is being carried live. It's a huge story. Everyone's falling all over themselves with the special report. There are lots of reporters, and there's a whole bank of microphones in front of the District Attorney. A group of serious looking men in suits stand behind the DA. The DA introduces all of them, and he thanks them for an effective investigation culminating in eliminating a terrible menace. Then he turns to the hoards of anxious reporters, who are practically salivating at something to add to their boring day.

DA: "Based on the suspect's DNA and other evidence, Greg Windor has been indicted on 16 felony counts."

Reporter: "What's the other evidence? Can you tell us now what you found in his house during the searches?"

DA: "At this time, I cannot answer that question."

Reporter: "Will Windor be charged with all 11 known DB25 crimes?

DA: "We have collected almost 1,000 pieces of evidence from three states during the DB25 investigation. Some of it is still being analyzed. A total of 180 officers from cities in three different states, as well as officials from the federal Bureau of Alcohol, Tobacco, Firearms and Explosives, and various state and county attorney's offices, have worked too hard for there to be any missteps now. Therefore, at this time, the charges against Mr. Windor are all related to the assault on Joyce Garlen. Further charges related to other assaults and murders are still pending."

Reporter: "So are you saying Greg Windor will eventually be charged with all of the crimes?"

DA: "The MO is very much the same in each of the DB25 cases, and we believe that charges in other cases could come."

Reporter: "Can the people in Arizona, Utah, and Idaho feel a sense of safety and justice now?"

Mayor Sam Millard: (stepping in front of the DA) "Far too many victims and their families have been tragically destroyed by one man's wickedness. Today, because of so many law enforcement agencies' superb work . . . today, the voice of justice rings forth. We realize that his capture cannot and does not end the pain of those who have suffered at the hands of the DB25 Monster, but our citizens can believe that safety and justice will now prevail."

It's such a stirring speech, I almost want to stand up and clap myself, except the photos of the monster that fill the screen in the next few seconds are of my father.

"Dad!" I silently call to the man on the screen. And then another set of reporters in another place. Wait . . . that one looks familiar. It's Mr. Baron's office. I recognize it even before the caption on TV. If he's upset by what he's just heard, he sure doesn't show it. In fact, Mr. Baron, with a white-lettered caption beneath him identifying him as Greg Windor's lead attorney, calmly says, "My client is pleading not guilty. After all the fancy speeches have died down, and after a trial in which justice finally occurs, my client will be found innocent of any and all charges. Like every other responsible member of our society, we are outraged by the DB25. We wish that law enforcement would focus on the real criminal before he strikes again instead of persecuting my client." Though reporters are shouting at him, Mr. Baron takes no further questions.

Our phone begins to ring and ring and ring. Reporters leave messages about how they'd like to reveal our side of the story. They'd like to know how we are feeling. They'd like to know if we saw any signs of the violence. They'd like to know if he was truly a Jekyll and Hyde. We don't answer.

It's a strange sense of déjà vu, only it's worse than Dad's arrest. At that time, I was in a complete state of shock. And since then, I've truly believed it was all a terrible mistake, but now that the DNA analysis has come back . . . now . . . despite what Dad's lawyer says, I know that my whole life has been one big lie. My father is not the man I knew, trusted, and loved. "Mom, I've got to get out of here."

"Kevin . . . please . . . think." I put on my sweatshirt. "Where do you need to go?" Mom says. She's hugging a throw pillow.

"I'll be okay," I say. "I'll avoid reporters. It's just . . . the walls are closing in. I'll be back."

I pull up the hood of the sweatshirt to partially hide my face. As if I'm some kind of criminal myself, I turn off the lights in the laundry room before I sneak out the back door, through the backyard and over the fence down the alley. I jog down the darkened alley for a couple of blocks. I'm not exactly sure where I'm heading, or maybe I do know. Twenty minutes later, I'm back home with a bag in my hand.

When I return, I overhear Mom on the phone. "Well, I can't just pull him out of school. And I'd have to have a job. We need money to live on . . . But I don't see how we can stay here . . . Right . . . I'll e-mail you all that. No, it's even worse than that. I know we go way back, but still thanks for everything . . ." I realize she's talking to Linda.

I walk into the bathroom with my new purchase and begin to read the directions. Half an hour later, there's a gentle knock. "Kev, are you okay in there?"

"Fine," I say.

"I made you some dinner."

"I'll be out in a few minutes," I call.

I'm not really hungry; I'm sure Mom isn't either, she's just trying to keep it together for me.

When I walk into the kitchen, my mom drops the spoon she's holding and gasps. "*What* did you do? Your hair . . ."

It's bright yellow—the color is pretty weird; maybe I didn't understand the dye instructions. But it doesn't matter; I shaved most of it off. No more dark hair hanging over my eyebrows like Dad's.

chapter 17

IT'S A WEEK LATER WHEN Mr. Baron calls our house. I answer, but Mr. Baron's secretary asks for my mother. I say he can speak with me.

The great Mr. Baron himself actually takes the phone insisting that he must speak with my mother. I want to argue, but what's the point? I hand her the phone and go pick up an extension. Mr. Baron asks Mom to come to his office. "She doesn't need to do that," I say, protecting her.

Mr. Baron ignores me. "If you'd like, you may bring Kevin with you."

"Can you tell me why you want to see us?" Mom says.

"I think that would be better handled in person," replies Mr. Baron in his usual don't-tell-anyone-anything voice.

I tell her she doesn't have to go, but she agrees to an appointment and hangs up. I walk back into the kitchen. "If he wants you to defend Dad, you don't have to do it. You don't have to say anything to that lawyer."

Mom says she'll be okay. I shouldn't worry. But I am. Mom is no match for that law firm. Neither am I, but at least I'll go with her and try to help her.

The news reports have been nonstop. They make me sick to my stomach. One long segment compares my dad to a guy called Dennis Rader—the BTK serial killer. I look him up on the Internet. *BTK* stands for blind, torture, kill, which is what he did to ten people. But right up until the time he was arrested, his wife and kids thought he was a good Christian and a good father. They'd grown up with him as a Cub Scout leader. His family never knew, never had any idea. Like me.

Mom may think Dad hasn't wanted to see me because he's protecting me, but I'm beginning to understand that the man I called my father doesn't want to have to look me in the eye and admit to being the monster he is.

Now what does his lawyer want with my mother?

When it's time to go to Mr. Baron's, I'm the one who leads the way. I've been here before—uninvited, but here. This time, I don't have to sit in the waiting area for a half hour or beg to be seen. This time, the receptionist ushers us into a small conference room. This time, she even asks if she could get us something to drink—a soda, a glass of iced tea. She says Mr. Baron will be with us in just a few minutes. Mom's fingers are gripping her purse. I try to calm her nerves. "Nice chairs, huh? Think they'd look good in our kitchen around the table? Maybe we could sneak a couple out under our shirts! What do they need with ten of them in here?"

Mom tries to smile at the stupid joke, but she's too nervous, and the smile doesn't look real. Funny thing is, I'm not nearly as nervous as I was when I came before. Then I thought my dad was innocent. Then I thought there was no way they'd ever find my father's DNA on a DB25 victim. Now, I'm just here because I know it's frightening for Mom. She lets so-called important people intimidate her even if they are jerks.

Mr. Baron enters the room. He's not a big man, not even as tall as me, but he gives off that I'm-somebody-special vibe. He bows slightly in my mother's direction and thanks her for coming. He reaches out his hand to shake mine as if we are old friends and says, "I see you've made some hair color and style changes." I don't respond, but he doesn't seem to care.

Mr. Baron takes a place at the table and opens a file folder he is holding. "Mrs. Windor," he begins.

"Her name is "Ms. Briggs," I interrupt. If he can't even get that right, how can he possibly remember all the facts in Dad's case? I fold my arms, ready to pounce on any other error, and then, I figure, what difference does it make? I'm done with my father. I'm only here to protect Mom.

The lawyer smiles. "Of course, forgive me, Ms. Briggs." He peers at his folder.

"What do you want?" I ask.

"Kevin, please," my mom shoots me a look. She thinks I should be polite.

The lawyer acts as if he didn't even notice my rudeness. He says that my dad has a favor to ask of my mother.

"A favor from my mom?" I interrupt. I can't believe it. She looks panicked. "Mom, it's okay. You don't have to be part of all this. Really, you don't."

Mom seems to be getting smaller in her chair. Mr. Baron says, "Your son is correct; you certainly cannot be compelled to do this, but please understand that Mr. Windor specifically requested your help."

That's it. I've had it. I beg to do something—anything to try to help, and my dad won't even see me. He's barely spoken to my mom for years, and suddenly, now that he's a criminal, he wants her assistance. "Well," I say to the lawyer, "You'll just have to tell my father that my mother is not going to help him."

The lawyer keeps a pleasant look on his face and continues as if he never heard me speak. "You see," he turns addressing only my mother, "Mr. Windor has become aware of the fact that under certain possible scenarios, his assets might be tied up for some time. Of course, such might not be the case, but in the possibility that such a thing might happen in the future, he prefers to make certain that his son is well provided for now. Thus, he has authorized me to create a trust fund for Kevin, and until Kevin is 25, he'd like for you to administer the distribution and use of that money."

"Me?" Mom says. We're both shocked.

Mr. Baron takes some papers from his folder. "Yes. Kevin's father believes that you and he both share the same desire for Kevin's life to be the best possible.

"Best possible?" I say under my breath. "Maybe he should have thought of that before he started killing people."

"Kevin!" Mom gasps.

I push my hands through the yellow fuzz on my head. "Mom, why not call it what it is. I've been so sure that Dad was a victim himself. But the DNA proves that I was wrong, doesn't it?"

Mom puts her hand on my shoulder. "Sweetheart, don't give up. Remember that Mr. Baron is pleading your dad not guilty."

"That doesn't mean Dad didn't butcher all those women. It just means that the DA has to prove it. Right, Mr. Baron? You'll get paid lots of Dad's money to confuse a jury or hope for a mistake, even if you help a killer to go free."

Mr. Baron's tone is frosty. "Young man, our entire constitutional justice system is founded on innocent until proven guilty. I am giving your father the defense to which he is entitled. Now, if you'd let me finish my conversation with your mother." He turns toward her. "Of course, you're welcome to have someone else look over all this paperwork if you wish, but it's quite simple." He lays some papers out in front of Mom. She looks at them.

"I . . . I don't think I understand," she says.

Mr. Baron: "What are you unclear about?"

My mother takes a deep breath. "Well, I'm sure I'm misreading this, but it looks like he's giving Kevin $750,000."

Mr. Baron nods. "Precisely."

"It's so much," Mom says. "I had no idea Greg was so rich."

"Actually, he'd like for it to have been more, but he could have a number of expenses that he hadn't anticipated."

Mom stutters, "I . . . I only went to high school. I didn't even graduate. I don't know . . . I mean, I haven't ever tried to handle . . . I mean I've never really had any money. I don't think I should be the person to take care of this." Mr. Baron explains that Dad was definite that she be the trustee. "He feels that no one would care more about Kevin or take better care of him. If you have any questions, you can always come back to this office for assistance, but Mr. Windor felt you would be the best person to spend the money wisely on Kevin. It is his hope that you will encourage Kevin to attend the best university to which he is accepted."

My father . . . just like his own father, I think bitterly. Their lives in pieces, and all they can worry about is their son attending a good university.

Mr. Baron tells Mom that Dad also wants her to have his car. Apparently, both of Dad's cars finally made their way to the police compound, and now, after having been thoroughly searched, they are being released. He hands her a card with an address on it and tells her that the paperwork has already been filed so that we need only show our driver's licenses to claim the vehicles.

"I . . . I won't take his car," Mom says, "but I will take care of it until . . . he's free.

I clear my throat. "I don't want his car, and I don't want his money."

Mr. Baron seems unfazed. "So, if you're comfortable with administering the trust, if you could just sign in these places." Mom reaches out and squeezes my hand, then she turns toward the lawyer and signs by the Xs. She puts the pen down. "Mr. Baron, if . . . if Greg truly is innocent, for my son's sake, get him out of this nightmare quickly."

Mr. Baron nods. "That's exactly what I plan to do."

We don't hear anything more from Mr. Baron. We make two trips to the police impound lot because we have to drive a car there to pick one up. The guy who releases Dad's Lexus checks his list, "Oh, yeah," he says, "the pervert's car." On the way home, Mom insists that we stop at Dad's place. She says she can't drive his Lexus, and we park it in his garage. I tell her I'm going to leave "my" car there too. She says it's different than her driving Dad's car, and she insists that I bring the Jeep home. I don't argue. But I leave the car in Mom's garage, where it sits unused.

After a few days, it begins to seem like a sort of stupid protest. Dad can't know whether I'm driving the car or not. My walking everywhere is only making my own life more difficult, and really, hasn't my father already made it hard enough?

So today, when I have to start my anger management class, I slide behind the wheel for the first time since before Dad was arrested. Kind of ironic.

I almost don't go. But showing up at this class is a condition of my not being expelled. Not that I care about school these days; I just don't think Mom can take anything more. I have to grow up. I've got to stay in school and out of trouble.

I check the address again and park in front of what seems like an old house. A young woman behind a desk looks up and smiles at me, "You here for the group meeting at 3:30?"

I nod, and she points me to what looks like a living room. There are three other teens already here. No one is talking to each other, and no one makes eye contact. I only recognize one guy. He's been in trouble since grade school. We've never exactly been in the same crowd before, but here we are. I name the guy next to him Tattoo Tom. He has practically no square inch exposed that hasn't undergone the needle, and he's got spiky red hair. I touch my own yellow fuzz. I guess I fit in after all. Two more guys enter and take their seats. Still, no one speaks. Still, no one makes eye contact. An old grandfather clock at one end of the room shows that the start time for this group is approaching. Five of us—guys. Don't girls ever need anger counseling? Guess not.

A woman walks into the room, welcomes us, checks a chart, and tells us we'll wait just another minute for two more to arrive. Almost on cue, a girl dressed in shocking pink from her hair, to nails, to lips, and even some eye stuff enters and perches on the edge of a straight-backed chair. And just as the group is supposed to begin, Lani strolls through the door. She sees me, looks startled for a second, and gives a slight shrug. Then she grabs two jelly donuts and plunks herself down on the floor.

The therapist introduces herself as Nancy, says we'll be meeting for the next six weeks, and has us introduce ourselves. People look so thrilled to be here—like sitting in the dean's office. She laughs. "Okay, so I know that no one wants to spend their afternoons with me, but you're here, so let's make it as painless as possible."

She tells us that we will need to understand and abide by the rules. "I hate rules," Tattoo Tom says.

"Fair enough," she says. "Most of us do, but we have to operate under them in here and in life. You can choose not to follow our group rules, but in making that choice, you'll have to leave. Decision is yours."

Pink-haired girl says that we can't leave, that we've been ordered to be here. Nancy smiles, "And by coming, you've followed the first rule. The rest aren't so bad either." She lists them: *What happens in this room stays in this room. You don't have to talk, but you do have to listen respectfully. No physicality and no profanity.* Fine with me. I'll keep my eyes open, but I plan to sleep through these sessions. I don't need anyone to help me understand my anger. Some dumb class where I talk to six other loser teenagers . . . no way that'll help with anything.

We play a couple of ice breakers that I remember from a long time ago in a church youth group. Guess they don't have any special get-to-know-you games for anger freaks. And then Nancy asks each of us to say in a very best-case scenario what would we hope to gain by having attended these classes.

Tattoo Tom says maybe it'll get his parole officer off his back. No one else speaks. Finally, pink girl, whose name is Becky, says she hopes maybe it'll help her get into a better foster home. Seems her outbursts scare them away. More silence. Nancy lets the quiet hang in the air. Lani sarcastically says, "Lots of free food," and she pops another donut into her mouth. Pretty soon, everyone has said something except me.

Nancy looks in my direction and waits, but I remain silent. Then Tattoo Tom speaks up, "Man, we probably already know why he's so pissed off." There's a murmer of agreement. Tattoo Tom, whose real name is Gerald, continues, "I got a lot of unfair crap in my life that really pisses me off, but I still guess I'm glad I'm not him."

And that's about the end of session one.

My cell phone rings. Hard to believe, but it's finally my grandmother. I haven't heard from either of them since I left, which means that they also haven't responded to the news about Dad's being indicted. When I answer the phone, Grandma's voice is warm. She tells me again how wonderful it was to see me. When can I come back? I'm always welcome. Nothing about my father. Finally, I have to ask. Do they know he's been indicted? They do.

"Are you and my grandfather coming in to talk to your son's lawyer, to see what you can do to help him?"

My grandmother sighs softly. "Your grandfather does not think that is a good idea at this time."

I hang up. I'm disgusted. How can they desert their son? I've given up on him, but that's different. Kids make mistakes; parents are supposed to be the ones to try to make things better. Did they

ever even try? I'm furious at my newfound grandparents. Another issue for my next anger management class.

I'm in the pizza lunch line at school. Jason passes
me. I don't make eye contact. Nothing new. We
haven't spoken for a while. But today, he stops.
"Hey, it's cool if you want to sit with us."
"Okay," I reply. But I head out to my spot alone
on the steps outside. It's just easier that way. I've gotten used to it. Today, I'm not alone for long. A kid
I've never seen before sits on the concrete step with
me. I ignore him. Probably just a dare to take a spot
next to the monster's kid.
"I'm Russ." I don't say anything. "I'm a sophomore." I still don't say anything. "I have a business
deal for you." I ignore him. "Okay, so I'm just going
to tell you about it because I think you'll like it." He
takes a bite of his sandwich and then continues.
"People think I'm a geek, but that's okay because I
do like computers. I've designed some great Web
sites."
I chew my pepperoni pizza staring straight ahead.
I'm not interested in his life's story.
"Geez, you don't make this easy. But I know we
can both make big bucks off this, so at least listen."
I wipe my face with my napkin and take a swig of

209

my soda. But he doesn't get the hint. He doesn't go away. In fact, he just keeps talking. "I want to set up a site, it'll have a live blog, but there'll be a lot more to it. All you have to do is add to the blog—every day would be terrific, but even a couple times a week is okay. We split all the profits, even if you only write like two paragraphs a week. Good deal, huh?"

I take another sip of my soda. I still haven't made eye contact. He still hasn't left. "Okay, so maybe you think I'm just a nobody, but I know what I'm talking about. You could get as much as $500 a week, maybe even more. Advertisers will line up for the hits we can promise them."

I could say that I don't need money. I'm already rich. $750,000. And it only cost me my life as I knew it. But I don't say anything.

"Fine," the kid says. "I'm just trying to help you make the most of this. I like making Web sites. This one, *The Monster's Son*, is going to bring a lot more hits if there's actually some stuff on it written by him, at least once in a while." He stands up. "Ignore me all you want, but try Googling your name. Do you know what's already out there about you? At least I want to give you a cut of the action."

chapter 18

I TELL MYSELF I DON'T care what that kid said. It's just some geeky underclassman trying to get noticed. But after school, I go home and Google my name. I can't believe it. Maybe no one is talking much to me, but they're talking plenty about me. Russ whoever is right. How can these people say these things? They don't even know me.

"I sat next to him our freshman year of Algebra. He'd get this weird look on his face—like maybe he knew his dad was doing terrible things to people."

"He's like the kids of that BTK murderer. The guy kept everyone in the dark; he was even involved in his church. That sicko led two lives. Kids didn't know. Bet Kevin didn't either."

"Everyone in our school is afraid of him. His eyes just lock on you until your skin crawls."

"I think they should kick him out. He looks like his dad, and he's gotta be like him on the inside too. Something awful is going to happen at our school. Everyone good is going to transfer if they don't kick him out."

"Remember that other kid, the one who's grown up now, but he wrote all those books about being beaten as a kid? Well, maybe Kevin is like that kid in the books. Maybe his dad's been abusing him for years. I'm pretty sure I've seen him with a black eye, and he's always got a lump or a bruise somewhere."

As I read on, the comments get even worse. "I think it's so great that you guys all know someone so famous . . . our school is boring, boring, boring . . . did I say mega-boring? How cool to have a famous killer's kid in your class! Dish more."

And the comments aren't on just one site. My name produces ten pages of sites. Stupid me. I thought that because I hadn't really been in the newspaper that much, I was under the radar except for people at school. Now, I realize that it doesn't matter if Mom can find another job or if we can move to another town. The World Wide Web will keep me visible, no matter how much I want to run away.

I wonder if Dad thought about any of this before he . . . and then I wonder what I'm thinking . . . that he worried about how it might affect his son's social life before he took a knife and carved up women.

I click on the next link. It's a victim's page, and apparently there are lots of comments from lots of victims of different crimes. I see my dad's name, and I read, "To Mr. Greg Windor: I just want to know why you did this. I am trying to forgive you. I am trying to think that it wasn't personal. You didn't mean to target my mom. You didn't mean for her to die. She wanted to live. She fought for almost two months afterward, and I know she is in a better place, but it's just so hard. My dad, my uncle, my brother; no one wants to talk about it. They think that'll be better for us all, but it just makes it harder for me. I wish I could sit down and talk to someone who could . . . well . . . I don't really know what anyone could do. I just feel so alone." She's signed her name, Melinda Alvarez.

I Google, and I find that her mother was one of the DB25's victims here in the Valley last year. A little more Internet research, and I see the girl lives in the Gilbert area. Not that far away.

I'm at the dentist's office, and he's running late. No sports magazines in the waiting room, so I pick up a *Newsweek*. There's a whole section inside about the mind of the serial killer. I'm not going to read it, but there are photos of famous ones like Bundy, Gacy, and Dahmer. Then I see one of my father, with a caption, "Suspected of as many as 25 different attacks on women in a tri-state area." I shut the magazine and drop it to the table as if I've been burned.

The dentist tells me I'm grinding my teeth, which is often a sign of stress. He writes a prescription for a mouthpiece and asks his receptionist to check and see if the pharmacy downstairs has one. She returns saying that this pharmacy is out, but their other store in Gilbert has the right size. She looks at me. "Would you like for me to have them send it over to the pharmacy downstairs?"

Gilbert. That's where the girl whose mom was one of Dad's victims lives. I look at the dentist. "I don't mind the drive. Just give me the prescription and the address." He does, instructing me it's important to get the mouthpiece to stop the grinding before I have real jaw problems.

Dr. Begley has been Dad's and my dentist for as long as I can remember, but he hasn't mentioned Dad today, and I'm certainly not going to. The dentist is halfway out of the exam room when he turns back to me and says, "I want you to know how sorry I am for you. I never had any idea about him either. No one could have known. No one. Not even his son. So try not to grind your teeth and blame yourself."

It's late, so I head for home, but all night I stare at the prescription in my hand and the Gilbert address of the pharmacy. MapQuest shows it's very close to Melinda's house. Maybe it would help us both if I could meet her and apologize for my father, for the horrible things he did to her mother.

A jury selection expert on TV says it's going to be very difficult to impanel an impartial jury for Dad's case. Based on previous cases Mr. Baron has tried, she feels that Greg Windor's defense attorney is one of the best. The expert feels certain Mr. Baron will try to get the trial moved to another state in which none of the crimes occurred. Motions and cross motions could delay the trial a year or two. And after that no-new-news item, the media leaves Dad and goes on to other current crimes and scandals. They'll be back with the "excitement" of Dad's trial, but I'll take the break from the spotlight for as long as it lasts.

Mom's friend Linda is still checking for jobs for Mom in Denver. There's nothing concrete yet. I think I'd just as soon stay here; at a new school, I'd be the curiosity factor all over again. I am still grinding my teeth, but I haven't gotten the mouth guard. No way I'm going to Gilbert without trying to see Melinda. But I don't know what I'd do if she opened the door, and she started screaming at my father's face. I want to tell her that we're both his victims, but I don't have the right to terrify her family any further, so I don't go. I just keep grinding away every night.

My life has a very different routine than the old Kevin Windor would have believed possible, but I make it through the day-to-day. I'm graduating from my anger management class. Lani hasn't been at the last two sessions. At the last one she attended, Nancy had switched from jelly donuts to peanut butter cookies, so I never knew for sure whether Lani had to attend or whether she really did just like the jelly donuts. Lani and me—we were the only ones who never said anything to Nancy or the group. But at least I stuck out the whole thing. I owed that to Mom.

After the last session, I hung around for a few minutes and asked Nancy about Lani, what happened to her.

"Were you two friends?" Nancy asks.

"Not really," I say. "We . . . uh . . . we had Chemistry together." I don't mention the night we talked on the curb.

Nancy looks skeptical. "Ahh, well, since you weren't friends, you probably don't know that Lani ran away."

"Geez," I blurt. "I thought she liked that group home."

Nancy folds her arms. "Well that's a fair amount of information from somebody who isn't friends with her. If you are in contact with Lani or do hear from her, it's pretty tough on the streets for a young woman. Encourage her to come back. I'll help her work out whatever the problem was."

"Okay," I say. I don't tell Nancy that I won't hear from Lani, that we were two lost people trying to get through one lonely Saturday night. I don't have a phone number for her; I don't even know if she has a phone. I tell myself that at least Lani's pretty tough. That should help her wherever she is; I just hope it will be enough.

Since I've followed the rules about completing my anger management class, I get the note I need to take back to school and meet the conditions of my continued enrollment at Chapparal High.

I think about how dumb I used to be. How despite everything, I kept holding onto the belief that Dad couldn't be guilty. How willing I was to ignore the evidence: the laptop he tried to hide from me, his taking my car when his wasn't even in the shop, his saying he was out of town when he was in Joyce Garlen's apartment, and his jail letter wanting to plead guilty. So why was I surprised when they found his DNA, when they charged him with the crime?

I don't need my father's money. Nothing can make up for what he did to those women. But I'll keep it for now. I'll make my own way in life, and when I'm really successful, I'll visit my father in jail, and I'll tear up a $750,000 check into little pieces.

I've started to study hard again. I'm going to need all the scholarships I can get. I'm pouring over my Pre-Cal book this afternoon when the phone rings. Caller ID says it's Mom at work.

"Kevin," there's a slightly frantic edge to her voice. "I'm driving home, and I just heard on the radio . . . turn on the TV." Her cell cuts out.

What now. Can't it ever just end? Why did I keep begging that lawyer not to let Dad plead guilty? If he had, Mom and I wouldn't have to suffer through being on trial right along with him and hear over and over and over again all the details of the horrible things he's done.

I squeeze my eyes shut for a second, and then I force myself to turn on the TV. Again breaking news fills the screen. Again the serious reporter staring out. "Speculation and rumors have been running rampant all day about this morning's murder. Police are now confirming that the woman killed had the same DB25 markings as the previous victims. We'll bring you more details as they emerge. Stay tuned to Fox News 10, where we bring you the news fast and first."

This makes no sense. My father is in jail. How could the DB25 Monster have struck again? I switch channels. There's a rerun of a sitcom, but only for a second, and then it, too, cuts to breaking news. Same basic report. I've heard it twice, but it still makes no sense. There can't be another victim of the DB25. They've already arrested him.

Mom gets home, and we sit waiting to hear what TV terrors we'll have to endure next. There's a breaking news report every twenty minutes, but most of it only rehashes the same few facts. The rest is crazy speculation until almost 9:30 at night. Then, just like at the first press conference, all the television stations have cameras and reporters, and the DA and group are once again facing them.

A police spokesman introduces himself and says he will be making the following statement. "At 10:00 this morning, the police were called to a home on East 75th Street, where they found the body of a 38-year-old woman. Her identity is being withheld until next of kin can be notified of her death. She had been bound, beaten, and slashed, and her body bore the DB25 branding. The deceased was found by her cleaning lady. At this time, that is all the information we are prepared to release, but within those confines, I will take limited questions."

Reporters jockey for position. "Is the MO the same as the DB25 Monster?"

"It appears to be similar, but we are not prepared to give a definite answer to that at this time."

"Is Greg Windor still in jail?"

"Yes."

A reporter shouts, "Then how do you explain this killing?"

"We cannot comment on that at this time."

The police spokesman looks grim as he ends the conference. But the television reporters have plenty they want to comment on and speculate about. Could there have been two different DB killers? Were they working together, or was one a copycat of the other? Finally, one reporter looks into the camera and asks, "Is it possible the real DB25 is still stalking the streets?"

The phone rings. My mom looks over at the caller ID. It's Mr. Baron. He wants to talk to us both. He says that no matter how much we are cornered, no matter how much we are tempted, we must remain quiet. "Don't let anyone goad you into a comment you'll later regret." But when I try to ask him what's going on, he says he can't discuss it with me and hangs up.

Mom and I watch TV all night hoping for someone to make sense of something. But instead, it's all speculation. Reporters on the late, late news and early, early morning news are filled with questions and comments, but they still don't know anything. After a while, they all sound the same. Except one. And that reporter's comment replays itself over and over in my brain. "Is it possible that all this time, the wrong man has been sitting in jail?"

But I who am my father's son, the person closest in the world to him, I have already convicted him in my mind. So if he's innocent, am I who gave up on him, am I the monster?

Over the next month things happen first very rapidly, then very slowly, and finally there is nothing. The day after the new attack, Dad's attorney demands that the police either reveal that Dad's DNA was found on any other DB25 victim or announce that it definitely was not. A week later, there is confirmation that Dad's DNA was *not* found on any other victim, but the police are quick to point out that they have not filed charges against him in any other crime. They still stand by the charges that a grand jury brought against Greg Windor in the attack on Joyce Garlen. Back to Mr. Baron, who says he is absolutely certain that his client will be absolved of that crime too. Mean-while, Ms. Garlen's comatose condition remains un-changed, and the only other surviving DB25 victims say that the monster's mask rendered him virtually unidentifiable.

I start calling Mr. Baron a lot. He doesn't even come to the phone. He has his secretary tell me that there's nothing to report yet. He will let me know when that changes.

I cannot stop thinking about my dad sitting in jail—maybe innocent. I tell myself that I tried to go see him; I tried to help him. He wouldn't let me. I tell myself that it's Dad's own fault I gave up on him. I go to school because it's worse to sit at home. I try to ignore rumors that some Web site has photos of me and Dad side by side with a caption that asks if Monster Junior took over after Monster Senior was jailed. Supposedly, there's even an online poll where people can vote on whether I was the one who killed the latest victim. I half wait for the police to arrest me. But the police don't even come to question me.

And, strangely enough, school goes on like all these terrible things aren't even happening. I'm sit-ting in Chemistry when I feel my phone vibrate in my pocket; there's no way I can take it out to see who's calling because it's been made very clear to me that I will have *no* further kind of infraction for anything this year—and cell phones are against the rules.

I ask for a bathroom pass. Mr. McBee isn't pleased. "You'll owe me five minutes after school if you can't wait."

I nod, take the pass, and hurry into the stairwell. No one is around, so I pull the phone from my pocket. I hope everything's okay with Mom. I flip it open. There's a voice message. It's from Mr. Baron. "Jared Johnston is being taken into custody, arrested for all of the known DB25 attacks."

Jared Johnston? But that's my father's boss.

chapter 13

HIT DIAL BACK ON my phone. The law office answers. I don't even wait for the laundry list of names but interrupt, "It's Kevin Windor. I need to talk to Mr. Baron immediately." The receptionist tells me that he's not in, can she take a message? "But he has to be there. He just called me on my cell phone. I need to talk to him now." The receptionist says that she cannot help me. She's sorry, but Mr. Baron isn't in.

I hang up. I call Mom at her work. Her voice mail answers. I feel like I'm going to pass out, I'm breathing so hard. Should I run down to the dean's office and tell her I have to turn on TV? Should I just go home? Then I stare at my phone. "Stop! Think!" I tell my shaking fingers to get on the Web. A few more keystrokes. There it is. "Startling development in DB25 case. Jared

Johnston, 54, general manager of Environ Computers, arrested. New grand jury reconsiders charges against alleged attacker Greg Windor. Charges dropped. Windor to be freed." I stare at the words I thought I would never see and sink to the ground in a mixture of intense relief, excitement, disbelief, and disappointment in myself for doubting him.

I want to be there when my dad walks out of jail. I want to apologize, even if there is no apology good enough. But Mr. Baron is firm. My father absolutely does not want that, and hasn't he been through enough? So like the rest of America, I watch on TV as my father walks out of jail a free man. Reporters shout questions at him, at Mr. Baron, at the police, but my dad just looks up at the sun, the sky, and he smiles. Then he gets into the back of a waiting black sedan with Mr. Baron, and they leave.

Like everyone else on the planet, we are glued to the official news conference about the new DB25 arrest. All the same players as for my dad's arrest are now again assembled for this news conference. The same man comes to the microphone. He says that they found Jared Johnston's DNA on all 11 of the known DB25 victims. He says that further investigation has revealed that Johnston traveled to each of the cities where the attack took place on or before the date of the attack, and that he had returned home shortly thereafter. A search of Johnston's home produced the DB25's mask.

The reporters ask about Dad's DNA. All the District Attorney says is that additional investigation has revealed that it was present on only one victim, but Dad has never denied being at her home, only that he had committed any crime there. Despite all the other unanswered questions, the news conference ends.

Mr. Baron calls to say Dad wants to meet with me and Mom. He doesn't want to do so in the glare of the media or the invasiveness of even one snooping reporter. That's not going to be easy to avoid. So Mr. Baron says Dad is going to an undisclosed location for a few days, and he'll get Mom and me there after the press is no longer camped on our doorstep.

The talk shows and the gossip columns are filled. Our home phone rings night and day. The principal has to threaten a couple of reporters with arrest if they return to campus with their cameras or their microphones. If the story of Dad's initial arrest was big, this is huge. Have the police suddenly found the real DB25 attacker? If so, why was Dad in that apartment that night, and why was he trying to escape through a window? The police will only say that Mr. Windor is no longer a suspect of a crime, nor is he a convicted felon. Therefore, as a private citizen, he has no duty to explain his actions.

At school, some kids come up to tell me that they're happy for me that Dad was freed. A couple of guys say they remember when my dad was their coach. He'd been a real good guy. Now they remember! But who am I to berate them? He is my father, and hadn't I given up on him? Lots of kids and even teachers are curious. Some hint, some ask direct questions. I say that I haven't seen my father since his release, and I only know the same things they know. I don't think kids believe me, but it's true.

Some in the media use Dad as an example of what's wrong with our judicial system. There's a long rant on the radio about what would have happened if Jared Johnston hadn't committed another crime. Would an innocent man's life have been ruined? Then there's a counterpoint where a guy keeps saying, "Where there's smoke, there's fire. Greg Windor maybe wasn't the DB25, but he was doing something real wrong."

But then the reporters begin to fade away as does Dad as the hot topic for talk radio. Jared Johnston, he's the story now.

Each day, we wait to hear from Mr. Baron about seeing Dad. Finally, Mr. Baron calls and says that

Dad has quietly returned to his condo, and he'd like for both of us to go see him this Saturday around noon. But before I see my father, I have to understand something. "Mr. Baron, my father was innocent, so why—why did he confess to such a horrible, horrible crime?"

"I don't expect I'll be speaking with you again, Kevin, and you didn't ask for it, but people pay me a lot of money for my advice. This time I'm giving it to you for free. Your father is not the DB25 killer. He's free. Enjoy your life and your time with him, and let the past few months go."

The week drags and speeds by at the same time as I think about Saturday. When we pull up to Dad's, I walk with Mom to the front door. I have my key, but somehow, it doesn't seem right to use it. We ring the bell.

Dad opens the door, but he stays behind it. "Sorry," he says, "Come in. I've gotten a little wary of the paparazzi."

He has lunch ready for us. Cold cuts and salads—the works—all set out in the kitchen. And there are three places set at the table. "My goodness," my mother says. "You shouldn't have done all this."

Dad smiles. "I didn't. Kev can tell you. I never cook. I just ordered this all in from AJ's." Then there's this awkward silence. We are all eyeing each other uncertainly.

"Well, everything looks delicious. Let's have lunch," Mom says. Good old Mom. Trying to keep things pleasant.

So we all take a plate of food and sit down at the table, but none of us really says much of anything, and it's clear that no one is much in the mood to eat. I glance at my dad without appearing to stare. He looks different somehow. He's lost a lot of weight, but it isn't just that. There's something that's changed about him.

Mom and Dad try to make small talk. I answer when I'm directly spoken to, but there's such a big lump in my throat, and I hate myself so much that I can't pretend that everything is okay.

Finally, Dad pushes his plate away. "Sorry. I guess this wasn't such a good idea. I . . . I just wanted to tell you both how sorry I am. I can only guess how tough the last few months have been for you both. I really did do everything I could think of to keep you out of the spotlight, but from where I was, I couldn't do very much."

Mom looks at Dad. "I tried to explain to Kevin that you didn't want him to visit you so he wouldn't be in the middle of the storm." I can tell she's choosing her words carefully. "I appreciate your caring so much about our son at what must have been the low point of your own life."

Dad says that he wants Mom to continue to be the trustee of the money he has set aside for me. And it's just a small apology, but he wants for her to keep his car. She says that she cannot do that. He leans over and looks into her eyes. I feel as if I shouldn't even be there. "I've put you through way more than was ever fair. I can't go back. I can't redo either of our lives. I owe you for the college degree I got and you didn't. The least I can do is to give you a decent car to drive. You don't have to take this one. You pick it out. New. Whatever you want. Let me do this one thing."

Mom has tears running down her cheeks. I think she's still going to say no, but to my surprise, she doesn't. Dad walks over and hugs me before Mom and I leave. He puts a silver object in my hand. "So many people have been in this house in the past few months, I changed the locks. Here's your new key. Use it any time."

I kind of pull away, and I shove the key in my pocket. He looks at me and nods. "It's okay. I understand if you just need some time."

I suppose if this were some movie, Dad and Mom would get back together now, and we'd all live happily ever after. But real life isn't so much that way. Mom does get a new car, her first one ever. She says people like her don't drive a Lexus. Besides, she has to afford the gas. Ultimately, she accepts the gift of a bright blue Prius. After the car comes, Mom and Dad really don't talk with each other again.

Mom begins encouraging me to return to spending some weekends at Dad's. Pretty ironic. She was the one so jealous every time I used to stay at his place, and now, she's the one sending me there. I shrug off her encouragement, but she doesn't let up. "Kevin—imagine how awful jail must have been, how much it would have helped him to see you. But he didn't let you come. He wanted to protect you. You mean everything to him. I think you're the only person in his life who has ever really mattered. He cares too much to ask you to come back, but you can't desert him now."

I can't explain to Mom. I don't even try. And every once in a while, I even tell myself that maybe I'm not so terrible for having given up on Dad. I mean, if we were supposed to be so close, how come Dad lied about going out of town when he was going to Joyce Garlen's? And what about that letter he had Mr. Baron give me? Did Dad really only write it to try to avoid a trial that would impact me? Some small warning in my brain tells me that it doesn't make sense.

231

But asking and re-asking myself these questions does not make me feel any better. In fact, I feel worse . . . I feel like I'm trying to find some loophole to justify my giving up on my father. I finally convince myself that for his sake, maybe Dad never has to find out I am a horrible person. I have to pretend to be the son he deserves because he deserves to have that son.

I'm headed over there to spend the first weekend since Dad's arrest. I'm dreading it. It's going to be so awkward.

And it is for the first few minutes. But then Dad acts like it's just another weekend. We don't have any heart-to-heart talks; we don't mention anything about the past months. We start playing this new computer game, and the hours fly by. I actually have a good time, and Dad says it was a great weekend. Right before I leave, Dad mentions that he's resigned from his job, so he won't be traveling anymore. I guess that makes sense. How could he go back there?

"Are . . . are you going to stay in Phoenix?" I ask. "Or will you have to move to get a new job?"

Dad says that he doesn't plan to work at all for a while, so he'll be around. "But you . . . pretty soon, you'll be taking off for college, so maybe your Mom and I can work out your staying here a little more before that happens."

I tell him I don't think that's going to work. I say it's because it would make Mom mad, but the truth is, the more time I spend with Dad, the more likely he's going to find out the truth about what a terrible kid he got.

He puts his arm around my shoulders, "Sorry. Your mom and I have always pulled you back and forth. All right, I won't even ask her." He punches my arm. "That's what you get for being such a great son. You're in high demand."

I can't stand it anymore. "I'm not such a great son. Really, I'm not. You deserve better."

Dad looks at me. "I don't begin to deserve a son as good as you."

chapter 20

TWO MONTHS PASS. EMILY and I still haven't spoken to each other. I'm not sure I would have even if she had apologized, which she still hasn't. She and Jason are still a couple, which means that even though he really has tried to restore our friendship, it doesn't work so well. Even though I didn't really know her at all, sometimes I think I had more in common with Lani. My crowd at school has no idea what it's like to have your whole life turn upside down in one day. Only I guess Lani's never turned right side up again. I wonder if she knows my dad is innocent? I hope so, and I hope that wherever she is, people see she's more than safety pins and burgundy and black.

As for school, Mr. Leonard has talked to the rest of my teachers, and they've decided, because of all I've been through, they'll give me incompletes in any subject I'm way behind in, and I can have the summer to make up work. That way, I can still apply to the colleges they think I want to attend. That was nice of Mr. Leonard. He really is a stand-up guy, but the truth is I no longer have any idea where I want to go. It doesn't seem so important.

My grandfather wouldn't be pleased to hear that. I called him the other day. I told him it wasn't too late for him to call Dad and tell him that he was glad that Dad was free. My grandfather dismissed the idea. He didn't want to hear anything about my father, he only wanted me to come move in with them; I told him no. So that was that. We've had no further communication, and my dad . . . he doesn't even know I've ever spoken to my grandfather.

One day, when we're out of school midday for some teacher meeting, I decide, that it would be nice to go have lunch with Dad. He's always alone. I wonder if he's ever going to get a real life back. I drive over and pull up on the driveway, glancing at a black sedan parked on the street.

I let myself in, and am about to shout hello, but then I hear Dad in conversation. I'm glad. He needs, deserves to have friends. Still, I'm curious who's here. No one has been around since, well . . . since before everything.

As I start toward Dad's office, I hear a man's voice

say, "Well, that's it then. All the confidentiality papers signed. Not bad. You must be a very wealthy man." The voice doesn't sound like anyone I know. *Who is it? What papers are they talking about . . . what wealth?*

I stop, trying to process what I've heard as Dad and two men walk out of his office. Shocked, Dad croaks, "Uh, my son." The two men say hello, walk to the front door, and leave. I look at my dad in expectation of more information, but none comes. "So . . . uh . . . aren't you supposed to be in school?" is all he says.

"Half day today," I answer. "Thought you might like company. Didn't know you were busy. Hope those guys didn't leave because of me."

I give Dad the perfect opening to explain about them, about what they said. But all Dad says is, "No problem. Hey, I found this little place that delivers the greatest sausage subs. Now we don't have to wait for the weekend for you to taste one. They're better than Tony's. I kid you not."

So no answer about the two men. And right up there with wondering about them are a lot of other questions I'd sure like to ask Dad. I'm so sick of all the secrets. But I, the son who was willing to believe the worst about his father—what right do I have to any answers at all? So I don't ask Dad what he was doing at that apartment, in that bathroom; I don't ask if it's just some weird coincidence that the DB25 turned out to be his boss, and I certainly don't ask what's so confidential or how or why Dad's rich now. I only say, "Sausage subs better than Tony's, no way!"

School's finally almost finished, but not quite. That's why I'm at Dad's today working on an impossible take-home English final. Why did Mr. Leonard decide to torture us with the Greek philosopher Homer for his final exam question? We'd all do a lot better if he'd let us discuss Homer Simpson. I read the directions again. "Choose one of these three famous quotes, explain it, and apply it to contemporary life in a five-page double-spaced essay."

I have both of Dad's computers running, but I'm getting nothing done. I can't even decide which quote to use . . . well, except the one about fathers and sons. My eyes go back to it again. I could write a lot about that, but just reading it makes me shudder. No way I'm using that one.

Shooting mini hoops from the executive basketball game Dad keeps on his desk seems like a much better idea than trying to write this final exam. I take the small ball and start making shots. Pretty good. I'm five-for-five. Then my next ball rings the basket, bounces on the desk, and falls behind it. There goes my streak! I crawl under the desk to retrieve the ball, but I can't find it. Finally, I think I see a little piece of orange; the ball must have rolled way back under the drawers. I stretch out full length under the desk and reach for it. Somehow I bang my head, and then something hits me in the face. It hurts. I feel the object that's fallen next to me and crawl out from under the desk with it still in my hand.

It's that same small gray computer I saw Dad using the night before he was arrested! What's it doing now in some kind of secret compartment under his desk? I turn it over in my hands. My heart is pounding. I fumble with the latch to get the computer open. I feel myself take a deep breath as I press start and wait for the screen to flicker on.

Nothing happens. The screen stays dark. The battery must be dead. A cord. There must be a cord to plug it in. I dive under the desk to see if it's in the compartment too. I feel my way until I've reached the spot. I stick my hand into the opening. No cord, but there seem to be some papers wedged in there. I yank on them and quickly crawl back out with them in my hand. What if Dad finds me rifling through his secrets? I don't even look at the papers. I shove everything into my backpack. I have to get out of here and find a way to get this computer running.

I don't even know exactly what I said to Dad, some lie about leaving a book I needed at Mom's or at Jason's or at another friend's, and it might be a few hours until I can track it down. I don't remember what Dad said in return. All I know is that I am out of Dad's house with my backpack and its hidden contents. The straps feel like they're on fire in my hands.

First step. A cord. I've got to get the thing to turn on. I step on the gas and head for Fry's Electronics. When I show a bored salesman my laptop, he shrugs, says they don't carry that brand so he can't help. Why can't anything just be simple?

I'm wracking my brain. This sales guy's no help at all. "A battery then. Can I get a new battery and charge it somehow?"

The sales guy barely even glances at the battery. "Sorry. Looks like it's only made for this computer."

"Please! I have to get stuff from this computer, right now—don't you have any suggestions?"

The salesman shakes his head. "Try the Internet or e-mail the manufacturer."

"Great," I say. "You don't have any other ideas?"

The salesman shrugs again. "Maybe that guy can

help you. He's been here longer than me." Without much hope, I walk over to the new guy.

"Nice laptop," he says. "Never seen one quite like it. It sure is small." He examines the back and shakes his head. My heart sinks. I reach out to take the laptop back, but he keeps staring at it. Then he reaches for some cords. "Maybe . . . if we put this in this and loop it in to this . . ." I totally lose what he's saying. All I know is that when he gets done, he takes one end of the three cords, plugs it in the wall, and the other in the computer, and the screen springs to life.

"It's not a real pretty way to do it . . . I'd still buy the required cord, but . . ." I don't know what else he says because I've already shouted a thanks and gone to pay for the cords.

"Maybe there's nothing here. Maybe there's nothing here," I keep repeating. But I don't believe a word I'm saying. This computer has to have explanations on it. It has to. Why else would Dad have hidden it under his desk?

I pay and I'm out of the store, but now what? Where to go to plug it in? I can't risk Dad's. Mom's is too far away. I need electricity and privacy fast. I get in the car and start driving, where I'm not sure until I spot a library on the left and pull in. The librarian says they have two private study rooms with computer spots. Both are full, but one has only ten more minutes of reserved time. "You can sit down while you wait," she offers. But she's wrong. I can't sit. The answers to the biggest puzzle of my life could be waiting right here in my hands. Do I want my dad to be a really good guy and me to be a horrible son, or do I want my worst thoughts confirmed about the father who is a monster? Either way, don't I lose?

Part of me wants to walk out of the library and forget getting onto the computer. But that part loses. I watch the clock tick off minutes to my turn—the room is mine for one hour. I set my backpack on the table, withdraw the small computer, the papers, and the makeshift cord. First the computer. If my time runs out, I can always read the papers in the car.

My hand is shaking so badly, I can hardly get the computer on. The screen springs to life, and I see that there are hundreds of files. But as I skim the titles, they're nothing more than the same games we like to play on Dad's regular computers.

My heart drops to my stomach. I have stolen my father's computer, lied to him, distrusted him, and for nothing. What's wrong with me? Why can't I just leave things alone? Why can't I stop looking for answers to questions that don't need them?

I put my head in my hands. I close the computer

and pull out the sheaf of papers from my backpack. They're probably just junk too.

They are pieces of lined notebook paper, and in my dad's handwriting on every page in the same smudged pencil are the words, "*Kevin is safe. Kevin is safe.*" That one sentence fills line after line, page after page. Why? When was I in danger?

I open the computer again. I don't know what I think I can find, but it's all I have. This time I start actually opening the files, one by one. It is a tedious process, and each file is exactly what the title indicates that it would be. I look at the clock on the wall. One hundred files down. This is pointless. But I have a half hour more . . . so I open another file and another and another. Then suddenly under the title *Road Control*, an old game we used to play, comes up some kind of spreadsheet that has nothing to do with the game. There's a list of dates, money borrowed, investments made, money returned, money made. It goes back for more than a few years. Is this my dad who is making all these investments? It looks like they've gotten bigger and bigger, and whoever made them has made a lot of money. The last one was just this year. Hard to tell where the money was borrowed from. It looks sort of like it was from Environ, but I think they're just a computer company, not a bank. I stare at each spreadsheet carefully. There's nothing else there, at least that I can understand. I guess it's no big deal to keep track of some investments, but if Dad had all this money, why did he have to keep working and traveling? Why couldn't he just stay in town and let me live with him? And why is all this stuff filed under some dumb computer game on a computer hidden in a secret compartment under his desk?

I close that file and start another bunch, hoping that the next one will bring answers. But none come. Again, each file is exactly what it's labeled. I have only ten minutes left. *Monster Truck Rally*. That's a game Dad and I have never played. I haven't even heard of it. I click the file open. There are no trucks, no road rally instructions. The screen fills with a document labeled Doing Business. I open it. It says Doing Business #1, then lists a city, state, company initials, and comments. The comments for #1 say, "Not much of a challenge—clearly recognizes the superiority of my product." Doing Business #2 has another city, state, and set of initials. Comments read, "Somewhat tricky. Error code ultimately corrected." The last entry indicates a Doing Business right here in town, a date, and there's even a street address on this one with company initials of JG. There are no comments.

I stare at the screen. It looks like Dad was keeping

track of the computer repairs he did for companies. Why is that a big deal? Why try to camouflage it under a game title?

It makes no sense . . . unless . . . no . . . *doing business* DB. Probably just a coincidence. The last entry has company initials of JG—I look again at the date next to it. That date. Forever burned in my brain because it was when my father was arrested. And the initials . . . I understand them now. JG—Joyce Garlen.

I feel as if I've been socked in the stomach. I can't catch my breath. I look away from the computer. It's too painful to look at it. Is my dad keeping track of his conquests? It can't be. I make myself turn back to the computer, and my fingers press onward. There's got to be another explanation. My dad can't be the DB25! They proved it because that monster struck again after Dad was in jail. But these entries end before Dad went to jail. Are there two DB25s?

I check some of the initials from the entries with news stories about the DB25's victims. The initials fit some of the victim's names, but not all of them. And there are more initials here than victims. Does that mean there are victims the police never discovered? My head is spinning. I feel sick.

The librarian knocks on my door and says, "There's someone waiting for this room."

I tell her I'm almost finished, hoping against hope that somehow in these last two files, there will be something that explains what I've seen beyond the truth of what it has to be. But the files are just the games indicated by the title. I close the computer, shove everything back in my backpack, and walk out.

I'm in a daze. The two men at his house . . . the one saying that Dad was a very wealthy man, the car he gave Mom, and the money he put in trust for me. Where did all that come from? Did he steal it from his victims? But the papers never said anything had been stolen. Who were those men? And who, really, is my father?

chapter 21

PULL IN TO DAD'S driveway. I don't know why I
have returned or what the right thing to do is from
here. I do know that even though he is my father, I
cannot let a killer walk free.

"Glad you're back," Dad calls as I walk in the
front door. "Did you get the book you need?" He
doesn't wait for an answer. "Tell you what . . .
how's this for motivation? Finish that final, and
we'll go see that new sci-fi movie that opened yesterday."

Something snaps inside me. But I can't seem to get
my voice to work, so I walk into the den, reach into
my backpack, and withdraw the small computer and
the sheets of "Kevin is safe." I place everything on
Dad's lap.

At first there is just silence. "Where . . . where did

you get these? Dad asks, and without waiting for an answer, he says, "How long have you had my computer?"

We both know what he's asking. "I booted it up. I read the files."

Dad bites his lip. "You saw both files?"

I nod. I put off asking about the worst of it because then I'll have to call the police. So I ask about *Road Control.*

Dad sighs deeply. "*Road Control* is a record of money, when I borrowed it from Environ, how I invested it, the results, and when I 'returned' the money I borrowed."

I'm thinking about murder, not money. But I only say, "So why's it a secret to borrow money from your company?"

Dad looks away. His voice is soft. "Because I got my loans by hacking into the computer system and taking the money. In legal terms that's called embezzling."

My head is reeling.

"I don't understand, Dad." They're the only words I can force out.

Dad puts his head in his hands. "No, I'm sure you don't. I never wanted you to think of your dad as a criminal. I didn't set out to become one."

"Why did you do it?" Dad has to know what I'm really asking him. I'm not talking about taking some money; I don't care about that. I'm asking about the killing.

Dad shakes his head. "It's complicated. My father never wanted a son, just a puppet. For most of my growing up, I danced on strings, doing everything he ordered, but finally, when he ordered me to break up with my first real girlfriend, I snapped. I wanted to show him that I was a man. No small rebellion would work with my father. I had to make a really grand stand." He looks up at the ceiling and then continues, "My father was completely stunned when I showed up as a married man and a father-to-be. However, he snapped out of it real fast and kicked me out. And I, the supposed genius—lacked money for food and rent for my pregnant wife and myself. So, I went back to my dad and begged him for help. He shut the door in my face."

I wonder how he can go on about this. What difference does it make? Nothing can justify what happened to those women. "Dad," I start to interrupt. He hears the anguish in my voice.

"I know," he says. "Despite how disappointed you must be in me, I don't want all this hanging between us. I don't want it to be the unspoken part of every conversation, but I've got to tell it my way." He takes a deep breath. "Less than a month after your mom and I were married, I knew it was a terrible mistake,

but I couldn't abandon her or you. It was awful."
Dad begins fiddling with his watch. "Finally, I had
my college degree; your mom and I could both get
jobs. We could share you and go our separate ways.
And I thought I could finally prove to my father that
I had made it in spite of him. I got hired at Environ
Computers . . . it was at a lower level than I'd hoped,
but I figured I'd prove I deserved one of the top
jobs."

Dad continues. "I worked hard and thought promotions would come, until Jared Johnston made it
clear that my education wasn't from the kind of
school that warranted a chance at a high management position. I started applying at other places, but
the great jobs . . . I just didn't have *the right*
education. So there it was—my father had won. I'd
not only thrown away his fancy university but the
kind of work I would have loved."

I cannot let my father go on talking about his
childhood. His father didn't make him murder anyone. Was my dad part of the killings? Did he and
Johnston plan them together? I open my mouth, but
find I cannot verbalize those thoughts. Instead, I am
only able to ask, "Johnston, were . . . were you two
partners?"

Dad snickers. "Hardly. When I tried to tell Johnston
that I thought there were flaws in our security sys-

tem, and I had some suggestions for plugging them, he informed me that he had a doctorate from MIT and didn't need any assistance from me.

"So one night, I was playing around on the computer, and I hacked into the company's accounting system. Got through all the cyberwalls, just to prove I could do it—to show myself I was smart even if they didn't recognize it. I waited to see if I'd get caught, but no one seemed the wiser. A few weeks later, I heard about an investment opportunity in a technology company. I knew it would be good, but I had no extra cash to invest. And then I remembered how I'd hacked into the company. I hacked in again and lent myself money to invest. It made a profit, and I repaid my loan. But it wasn't a big enough splash. Having made a little money, I wanted suddenly to get enough wealth to throw it in my father's face." Dad still won't look at me as he speaks. "So . . . I *borrowed* additional funds from the company. No one ever knew. I found out I was pretty good at investing. Eventually, I could have used my own money. But it became a game to successfully hack in and use the company's without being discovered. It didn't make it right, but I told myself it was okay because I always returned every penny I took. So, that's it. The *Road Control* file."

I can feel how tight my throat is. I have to hear it

from him to believe for certain what I already know. "And The *Monster Truck Rally* file and all those sheets of paper with my name."

Dad leans back on the sofa. "Kevin, can you take more? Do you already hate me?"

I don't answer. I only say, "The *Monster Truck* file."

Dad stands up and begins pacing. "One night, while I was hacking, I found Jared Johnston's locked files. He'd taken credit for a lot of my ideas. He always lorded his Ivy League degree over me; so just for the hell of it, I decided to see if I could sneak into his personal locked files. I wasn't even going to mess with them . . . it was satisfying enough just to invade his privacy." Dad runs his hand across his hair. "Funny how life is. I probably would have logged in one time and forgotten about it. But I did it the night after I'd watched a TV special on the DB25 Monster. And there was this one file that Johnston had that just didn't make sense. It was a spreadsheet. There were so many coincidences that even though it was unbelievable, it pointed to him as the DB25."

I interrupt. "So why didn't you just go to the police?"

"And tell them . . . what? That I'd been breaking laws by hacking into my company's locked files? That I'd happened on some private information while I was stealing money? Oh, yeah, and because of all that illegal activity, I had an idea that the DB25 Monster could be my boss, the same boss who kept turning me down for promotions?"

Dad shakes his head. "At best, the police would have thought I was a nutcase. At worst, I'd have lost my job—maybe even landed in jail for my own illegal activities. So I downloaded and hid Johnston's files onto my little computer; I went over and over them; he could have been the DB25, but the files didn't absolutely prove it. What if it was just a series of coincidences and I was wrong? What if Johnston turned out to be innocent after I'd accused him to the police? He'd have made certain I paid in a big way."

Dad continues, "But what if I was right? I just couldn't let women continue to be murdered if I knew who the monster was." Dad keeps pacing and talking. "If you looked at *Monster Truck*, you saw that Johnston's notes became much more detailed for JG than anyone else. It was the first time he gave a street address, and it was even nearby." Dad sinks back onto the sofa. "God knows why I thought I should or could do this . . . too many TV cop shows I guess, but I decided that the most logical thing for me to do was stake out that address on that night. I thought I was being smart. I wasn't going to confront Johnston. If he showed up, I'd call 911. The police would come; the woman would be safe; the DB25 would have been caught and behind bars, and all my illegal breaking into computers would remain my secret."

So my father wasn't the DB25. He hadn't killed anyone. Before the relief about Dad or the disgust at myself can fully penetrate, Dad continues. "I guess deep down, I didn't really believe it could be Johnston despite what I'd read in his files. I'd worked for him for years; he was a know-it-all jerk, but not a murderer.

"As I tell it to you, it all seems so stupid, but at the time, I thought my idea for a stakeout was both reasonable and careful. I congratulated myself on thinking it through enough to have borrowed your car so that Johnston wouldn't recognize mine."

"So, I sat in the cold, dark car and waited outside Joyce Garlen's apartment, but nothing happened. Finally, I guess I must have dozed off because I didn't even hear the car door open. All I know was that suddenly, I heard someone saying, 'Get out very quietly and very slowly.' My eyes flew open to see Jared Johnston with a gun pointed at my head."

"Oh, Dad!" I gasp.

He continues as if he didn't even hear me. "I did what Johnston said. As we walked toward that woman's apartment, I could feel the gun in my back, and I was desperately trying to think how I could save her and myself. I was praying that her door would be locked, that someone would see two strange men approaching. But no one was around. Johnston, with one hand still holding the gun to my back, used some kind of tool in his other hand on the door lock, and we were inside the apartment."

Dad's voice is ragged. "The next thing I remember was lying on the floor there. I couldn't move, but I saw Johnston standing over Joyce Garlen's beaten body. Then he walked over to me, laughed and welcomed me back to consciousness. Said he'd been waiting too long to fill me in on everything. He'd discovered my visits to his locked files, and watched as I started deciphering his other life. He was glad. He thought it added to the excitement. He'd figured I'd fall for the Joyce Garlen trap he'd created. Once he'd gotten me into her apartment, it had been easy to drug me. He was only sorry that I'd passed out and missed a master doing his work. He wanted me to know that while I was "sleeping," he'd dragged my body over to hers and scraped my face with her fingernails hard enough to draw blood.

I can hardly believe what I'm hearing. That's why the DNA they found on that woman was Dad's! I'm too stunned to speak.

Dad continues. It's as if once he's started, he cannot stop until the whole terrible story is told. "I was still so groggy and unable to stand, but I told Johnston if he killed me, there was a hidden computer file. When the police investigated my death, they'd uncover it and figure out who the real DB25 was."

Dad puts his head in his hands. "You know what Johnston did? He laughed. Said I'd added so much fun to his games, he wouldn't dream of killing me. Instead, he dragged me into that poor woman's bathroom and dumped me on the floor. When my legs would finally support me, I tried to climb out the window to go get help. I was afraid that if I went out the door, Johnston might still be there and stop me."

I'm trying to sort all this out. "But after . . . after you were arrested, why didn't you just tell the police about Johnston? Why didn't you show them how to get to your little computer with the hidden files? Even if you'd gotten in trouble for embezzling, it would have been so much better than being thought of as a killer. Why did you tell Mr. Baron you were going to plead guilty to being the DB25?"

Dad bites his lip. He doesn't answer. I look at the papers on his lap. "Me?" I ask incredulously. "How do I fit into this? Tell me," I demand.

Dad takes a deep breath. "When we were in the

apartment, Johnston showed me the photo I kept of you on my desk. Said if I tried to implicate him in any way, you'd be dead before the police ever found him. I looked at that poor carved-up woman, and at Johnston's expressionless eyes, and I knew he would do it."

I feel as if someone has hit me in the gut. My father was going to confess to the most brutal of crimes because he thought it would protect me; he was willing to spend his life in jail, and me . . . great son that I am . . . I was ready to believe he had committed atrocities.

We both sit in silence. Hating myself, I'm trying to digest the enormity of the sacrifice my father was willing to make for me.

Then Dad starts talking again almost as if he's thinking aloud. "Johnston had won. I wasn't going to tell. I'd go jail. And you would stay safe."

"But the police—they could have protected me and Mom."

Dad shook his head. "I wasn't willing to bet your life on that. This was a killer who had evaded how many police departments in how many states? This was a monster who enjoyed torturing and killing but was able to function so normally that no one suspected him.

"I thought once I'd gone to prison, Johnston

might enjoy having gotten away with all those murders, but at least, he'd be done. He wasn't stupid. He had to know that as long as he didn't kill again, he'd be safe. The DB25 was already behind bars. No one would be looking for him. And that meant you would also be safe."

"But then later Mr. Baron said you were pleading not guilty."

Dad nods. "Yes, he is a very persuasive man, and he said that even though I wouldn't help him with a defense, and I refused to testify, I might still get off because the state had to prove I was guilty. He said it was worth a try and that they might not have enough evidence for a conviction. I decided that since I wouldn't implicate Johnston in any way, or even say I wasn't the DB25, he wouldn't hurt you. Jail was so awful. I wanted to believe Mr. Baron that maybe somehow the state would make a mistake in the prosecution, and I'd be freed."

"But . . . then Johnston killed another woman," I say.

Dad nods. "That's when I realized it was never going to end—Johnston was going to keep killing unless I made the police understand the truth and helped them to capture him."

"And the police did listen to you!"

"Not at first. But they couldn't explain the other

killings. There were certain details that meant it couldn't have been a copycat. And the police had not found my DNA on any victim except Joyce Garlen."

"Dad . . . you stopped that monster. You're a hero."

He holds up his hand to silence me. "No. I'm a thief. I paid every penny back, but that doesn't excuse my stealing. I'm not in jail because many of those thefts are past the statute of limitations and because Environ is already reeling and wants no more negative publicity. Those people here today, they were the attorneys for the last of the confidentiality sign-offs. They won't prosecute. I won't ever work for Environ again, nor reveal to anyone except them the ways I broke through their system."

Dad won't look at me. "You wanted honesty. Here's honesty. I don't need a lot of money. But I risked everything for it. Why? All so that one day I could go back to my father and throw my great financial success in his face—so I could let him know I'd made it, and I didn't need him. He'd been wrong about me.

"Every sleepless night in that horrible jail, I'd think about how I'd be spending the rest of my life locked up, and I asked myself a million times, how different could my life have been if only . . ." Dad shrugs helplessly. "Kind of funny in a way. My life has been shaped by how much I've hated being my father's son and how much I've loved being my son's father." He wipes his eyes. "I'm sorry, Kev. So sorry."

The Homer quote Mr. Leonard gave us, I understand it now. "For rarely are sons similar to their fathers: most are worse, and a few are better." I look at my dad, and I wonder, *which kind of son am I?*

I see my father's pleading eyes, and I reach out to put my arm around his shoulders.

TERRI FIELDS is an award-winning teacher and author of over seventeen books. She also works as a reading and writing consultant, presenting workshops nationally and internationally to teachers about "Putting the Love Back into Teaching Language Arts."

Terri lives with her husband in Phoenix, Arizona.